Treasures

Book Three of the Mars Virus Series

Treasures

Book Three of the Mars Virus Series

by
Mark R. Sneller

Published by Fresh Air Press

Visit Mark's website at
marksneller.com

This edition was prepared for publication by
Ghost River Images
5350 East Fourth Street
Tucson, Arizona 85711
www.ghostriverimages.com

ISBN 978-1-7368917-1-1

Library of Congress Control Number: 2021918426

Printed in the United States of America
September, 2021

Other books Mark R. Sneller:

A Breath of Fresh Air

Greener Cleaner Indoor Air–a Guide
    to Healthier Living – 2nd Edition

Toxic Exposure

Dying to Read

The Mars Virus

The City Beneath the Earth

Strange Adventures

PREQUEL

In an attempt to look for life on Mars and against his better judgment, cancer researcher Jason Randolph scraped a few micrograms of dust from a meteorite his geologist friend had discovered in Antarctica. Authorities acknowledged the rock had come from Mars at some point in the distant past, not an unusual event.

Randolph added the dust to a few test tubes containing solutions he had flippantly created, considering the exercise to be fruitless. Only days later, noticing a red glow, Randolph removed the cotton plug from one test tube to check a sample using a microscope. That simple act unleashed The Mars Virus.

Yet, even as The Mars Virus ran rampant throughout the world, infecting the DNA of every living thing on the planet to cause mutations in each, Randolph found a way to harvest the outer viral shell, known as the capsid. He teamed with a brilliant engineer named Wilbur Gottlieb who used the shells to make usable products, from clothing to bulletproof armor, to flat panels for housing. All the while, plants grew faster, produced more oxygen, emitted more water vapor, and absorbed more carbon dioxide. All viral disease disappeared from every life form on earth, the viruses themselves infected by the virus from Mars.

Scientific experimentation using anything with DNA became impossible. This included test tube and Petri plate research where bacteria, fungi, algae, and plant cells were used. The virus could be found literally everywhere, on surfaces, in the air, and under water.

Thanks to this alien virus, the melting of the polar ice caps and the redistribution of water played a major role in affecting the wobble of the planet. The increased number of earthquakes and volcanic eruptions assisted in the distribution of energy. Seasons tended to meld into one another. Seacoasts disappeared, rivers and all water courses overflowed, and the weather of the day became unpredictable, in large part because there were no weathermen left to predict anything. The compass no longer had any meaningful relationship to north-south directions thanks to the shifting of Earth's iron core.

Intelligence increased among mammalian species that could now avoid hunters because they were more wary and quicker, flying creatures could fly faster and longer, fish could avoid bait, and humans could compute faster and became more athletic. Infected horses could run more swiftly, which caused the death of horse racing as a sport. Infected athletes could fun faster than non-infected athletes, which led to a temporary fascination in sports until geological changes caused by the virus brought an end to the fun, when competition to survive trumped competition for enjoyment.

Structural changes in the infected newborn became the norm. In the dog and human, shoulders were more hunched and thighs were thicker. The rate of learning increased. Because of the off-set nature of the eyes, ears, and mouth, the mutants earned the name of siders.

The Randolph vaccine put a stop to that and protected unborn children from becoming infected. In a desperate attempt to save mankind, Gottlieb constructed an underground city near Phoenix, Arizona, designed to house some 220 souls. Two decades later, earthquakes began to cause the city to crumble.

It was Jessica Galloway, an 18-year old born underground, who first went to the surface to explore the possibility that her people might move Topside. During her adventurous visits, Jess fell in love with a Topsider man, Carter, who showed her a different life, one that included both the ugliness and beauty of a surface world ravaged by storms.

On the surface, Jess also met Jay Whitmore, once a student of Jason Randolph, and his Chinese-born wife, Wei. Both befriended her and presented her with her own pup named Carla, a sider dog, faster than most, smart as a six-year-old child, and totally obedient.

Working with Carter's old military friend Ken and his wife, Beth, the team went all out to make a new home for those who fled UL-One, the city beneath the earth.

Carter and Ken were forced to enlarge a home site near Sedona, Arizona, to accommodate an influx of migrants from a decaying and rapidly dying city some 100 miles to the south.

Jess found her strengths and her weaknesses, as she struggled to understand a completely different world where self-defense and killing on the surface were as commonplace as were intellect and community spirit down below.

PART ONE

1

Added to the woes of trying to find a new home for any survivors, the upcoming poisonings, murders, drug abuses, and autopsies would prove to be confounding. Whether these were offset by the unfathomable riches yet to be discovered is up to question.

Jess stood at the entrance to the cavern, as it came to be known. It wasn't a true cavern, only a hollowed out section of mountain that Wilbur Gottlieb had created in his first and failed attempt to create a protected city. This occurred before he had constructed Underground Living Number One or UL-One (pron. Ulone), the city beneath the earth, located south of the remnants of Phoenix, Arizona. Over the course of years, the city suffered a number of traumas until earthquakes eventually led to its collapse.

Many long hours passed since Ken received the phone call for help from Danny Gomez, mayor and the only doctor remaining in UL-One, or probably anywhere, for that matter.

A score of locals began to clean and level the floor of the cavern, removing debris from the cracks in the rocks to permit good airflow, trying to make it livable. It had all been accomplished by lantern light. Outside, backhoed trenches had been seeded with powdered lime for the creation of gang-bathrooms. Beth, Ken's wife, worked with Annie, head of the greenhouses, along with numerous helpers to prepare enough food for several meals and to prepare sleeping spaces.

Ignoring the 10-15 mile-per-hour cool-to-cold wind that almost constantly blew down from the north, Wei met Jess as they exited the southern greenhouse, both serving their daily shifts. Wei asked, "You must feel terrible about the loss of your home," concern showing in her downcast mouth. Her sider blood not only gave the China-born woman greater intellect and physical strength compared with other humans, it also imbued her with a sense of greater empathy.

Jess gave a brief shrug, pushing her palms into her eyes, holding back tears, brushing back her red hair. "I have mixed feelings about the collapse. An earthquake destroyed my home. It's gone, never to be seen again. I want to remember it as intact and not what it looks like now. I used to view it as a repository for humans while the world went to hell. I guess it served its purpose, but it hurts to know that so many people I grew up with have been killed. I loved that city." At that, she began to sob.

Wei put her arm around her young friend's shoulder in an attempt to absorb some of that pain. *Share your pain, cut it in half. Share your happiness and double it.* At that moment, Carla stepped closer to her master and put her head beneath Jess's hand. Scratching her head, Jess recalled Carter's words when he had first presented the pup to her. *As a sider dog, she will have the understanding of six year old child. You can speak to her in complete sentences. She will be totally obedient, forgiving, and will do anything you ask of her, even kill if necessary.* Which, of course, she had done and will do again.

With great compassion, Wei said, "Honey, no two loves are the same. There will be plenty of loves in your life if you let them in, so don't mourn too much about a love you lost."

To pick up the survivors, the drive down necessitated going through the pass, a slow torturous drive, fraught with potholes, inclement weather, and unknown dangers necessitating a slow crawl in speed and time. The reward could be claimed at the other end defined as the saving of human souls who needed rescuing from a collapsing city.

As one of the earlier escapees from the city, Gregor pulled the U-Haul into the southern portion of low-desert earth demarking the location of the underground city, glad the long six-seven hour drive had ended. He got out of the truck. Carter slid out the passenger side.

Looking at the vultures circling overhead, Gregor stated the obvious, "It seems strange to bring this big U-Haul down here on a seven-hour drive only to pick up something that totals less than an ounce in weight and an inch in thickness."

The panels Gregor referred to measured 8' by 15' sheets of virus shells that Gottlieb had worked into flat layers to serve as separators between housing units. They were proof of everything: sound, light, radiation, and bullets. Much thinner than a piece of paper, each possessed the weight of a feather. They had survived millions of years in outer space. They were inflexible. They would never be created again. No value could be placed on them. To possess one would be worth a king's fortune, now they were slated to pick up several to add to those in their collection currently in use as wind shields and building components.

At that moment, Ken brought in the large yellow 92-passenger school bus to park next to them. He got out, stretching every limb and rubbing his backside. Dr. Alex Gomez, Danny's son, and his own late-teens offspring, Alex Junior, or A.J., followed him.

Carter first spotted Danny, the sole true surface-trained doctor left, seated against a pile of debris that once constituted the wall surrounding the city. At their arrival, the doctor stood and announced sadly, "We've got 52 survivors, and a dozen of them need serious medical attention; and Alex . . . your mother is gone."

"Mom gone? Only 52 left out of how many? That's it?" Alex exclaimed, astounded.

"Grandma?" cried A.J. "Where is she? Can I see her?"

"I'm so sorry," Danny said, putting an arm around his grandson. "It all happened at once. They're buried."

Speaking disjointedly, he rambled, telling them what he had already reported on the sat phone, "Our air is bad. We're eating leftover food."

Alex said, "Dad, we'll do what we can. We brought the splints, sutures, disinfectants, compresses, and other items you requested, so let's tend to them while we get the others loaded."

Danny pointed to his right on the ground, saying almost inconsequentially, "We pulled what panels could; maybe a dozen. You may be able to get more if you're willing to sift through blocks of concrete and re-bar."

"Are the survivors still below? I can't imagine that," Alex asked.

"No, they're up in the Pen," Danny replied.

The six men walked up the hill in the blast furnace of the Phoenix air, well into the 120s. Once in the Pen, the flat, shaded area outside the east exit to the city, three took the stairway down into the city proper to try and retrieve more panels while the other three remained to care for the wounded and bring the survivors down to the air conditioned bus that Ken left running.

With the assistance of volunteers, Ken, Gregor, and Carter—all big men— surveyed the remains of the collapsed tunnels, accessing areas of fallen ceiling that could be most easily removed in order to slide out any of the precious panels before further collapse buried them. With considerable effort and sweating in hot stale air, reeking of decomposing bodies buried beneath rubble, the men retrieved four more. The long panels were taken out the Pen door on the diagonal and carried down the hill to load them and their brethren in the bed of the truck. The three men, disgusted beyond measure at what they had seen during their digging and rock removal, made one last trip up the hill to assist survivors down to the air-conditioned bus, which carried ample supplies of water and food for the long and final journey northward.

"How many panels do you think are left down there?" Ken inquired, off-handedly, climbing into the driver's seat of the bus, after Gregor had ensured the refugees were secure.

"Maybe 80, I don't know, I can't think," Gregor replied robotically.

Ken thought, *The greatest treasure on the planet next door calling our name, begging to be ours and we can't get to it.*

2

A ring of red-orange boulders surrounded a portion their little community, Sekah City, an aberration of the name Jessica. Within the ring could be found a three-bedroom house, two trailers, the meeting hall, a greenhouse, a small front-end loader and barrels of diesel fuel augmented with xylene. Outside the ring just to the east could be found the parking area, residence hall, and medical center that now housed the Gomez family, doctors all, in a loose sense of the term. Across the river were located the turkey farm, a second greenhouse, and a larger trailer, as well as the cavern housing the last of the immigrants, some half-mile farther to the south.

Now a mother of two and mayor of Sekah City, Jess stood before a whiteboard mounted on the wall in the meeting hall. In front of her sat the entire city council. Her babies lay sleeping in a collapsible twin-stroller Jay had brought back from Flagstaff as a surprise.

Writing as she spoke, she said, "Using some of the panels recently brought back from Phoenix, together with standard brick and mortar construction, the capacity of the residence hall and meeting hall can be significantly increased. Weather is always the big variable.

"Jay, Wei, could you work up a design for both buildings?"

Both nodded their assent.

"Also, I want a better communication system. We have a single bell. I'd like to find a larger bell to develop a coding system that will communicate messages using both, such as emergency shelter, weather of the day, general meeting, gathering of certain groups, shift changes for meals, and so forth. I'll take care of that."

Jess continued, "As for food, since we stopped hunting to preserve the animal population, we still have fish, turkey, eggs, crickets, fruits and vegetables. Annie, the immigrants just doubled our population. How long can we feed them all?"

"Not long," Annie replied. "We're all going to have to eat less for a few weeks. We need to double our fruit and vegetable production immediately. This means expanding the size of one of the greenhouses, especially the one attached to the north side of this building."

"I'll meet with you on that later, mom. We can

plan it together," Gregor offered. "We'll have every-thing under control in no time."

Wrong thing to say, thought Carter.

3

The finding of the body confounded the two doctors who were totally unprepared to perform an autopsy. In their 20 years underground, they possessed neither the tools, experience, nor necessity to conduct one. In their previous life, any medical emergencies were called in for pickup by Ken, or one of his designated drivers, who drove down from Phoenix to the underground city, and who delivered the patient to the army base hospital, where they remained from days to weeks, and then returned. That is, until the entire military based was destroyed by a series of microbursts.

The body on the table in front of them belonged to Blondie, a 38 year-old woman married to the band director. Noted for her outgoing cheerful personality, she happily traded the latest jokes. After she failed to appear for her second-shift dinner, a search party found her dead, laying among the leaves of the forest near the residence center and covered with insects.

Upon the discovery of her body, a member of the search party summoned Jess, who returned with Carla, their dog. Word of the find spread fast and Brenda Russo met the small group as they exited the forest. In order to keep her out of trouble, Ken had assigned her to maintain cleanliness at the Big House, some two miles distance, when she was not on kitchen rotation.

Inspecting Brenda's handiwork at the house, Ken found himself impressed with her work effort and clearly, the entire house was cleaner than the one he and Beth had occupied for two decades in Phoenix. There were a number of reasons for this, but mostly because they lacked sufficient water and cooling to entice them to work. Here, Brenda must have felt she lived in a storybook paradise, in a palatial mansion. The two story home was infinitely better than the small cubicles in the residence hall where two beds fit in a room with a small desk, single chair, small dresser and some shelf space. Even the small unit everyone had occupied in the city beneath the earth paled in comparison. Here, she had it all. To no one's surprise, she occasionally stayed behind to miss a meal. So what if she had an occasional male visitor.

The year before, at the completion of the residence hall, Jess proposed a rotation schedule for the Big House that could accommodate 11 persons, with Brenda the only permanent residence, who served as the cleaning maid. In that schedule, each group of 10 would stay for two weeks, then return to the hall. This practice served as a psychological buffer to prevent jealousy of those living better than others and gave residents of the hall something to look forward to.

Exiting the forest and running face-to face with Brenda, Jess said, with all sincerity, "I'm sorry. I know you lost your best friend. I mean, we all loved her."

Jess watched Brenda, who displayed a look of surprise rather than the loss of a friend. It appeared as though Brenda fit into the large category belonging to those who suffered from adjustment-to-surface-life-syndrome.

The doctors poured over their small library of medical books for some clue as to Blondie's demise. For two days, she had been complaining of stomach pain and headaches. Even if they had the experience of conducting an autopsy, there existed no satisfactory physical space to perform it, certainly not on the single table used for minor surgeries, because of potential contamination of the surfaces and insufficient lighting.

Danny thought it would be a good idea if they hastily rigged a tent outside the medical center with a suitable table and lights with greater luminance. At the least, they might examine the contents of her stomach and small intestine. When they did so, all they found was the remains of undigested eggs, garden vegetables, and kiln-baked soy bread—exactly what everyone had eaten for breakfast. It told them nothing about what she might have eaten prior to the last meal. They lacked neither the experience nor the equipment to delve further.

Danny did find a few insect bite marks on her body which led them to the conclusion that, for whatever reason, she had missed her dinner and entered the forest, and she had failed to use enough bug-oil retardant. Therefore, the simplest explanation served as the answer. This was entered into her medical report: Some unknown species of insect had probably caused her demise. This might have begun days before when she first complained of symptoms.

After extensive discussion with the doctors, Jess issued the following edicts: No person shall go into the forest alone, to ensure their partner was well covered with the protective oil, and that manufacture of the oil be increased immediately.

Danny had a problem with his own conclusion. Pharmacology 101 says that symptoms tend to match the method of contamination. Blondie died from a digestive tract irritant, not from insect bites, respiratory irritant, or contact dermatitis. This irritant got absorbed to cause everything from severe drop in blood pressure to organ failure.

Two weeks after Blondie's death, in mid-morning, while completing construction of the newly enlarged residence hall, Jacob Jorgensen began singing. He felt excited about working outdoors and in his euphoria and enthusiasm, dropped a heavy cinder block on his foot and broke it. Broken bones were not uncommon among those who worked construction outdoors for the first time in their lives;

however, in Jacob's case, he blamed it on an occasional paralysis in his arms. These were preceded by digestive issues.

A single week following Jorgenson incident, a married woman walked into the rapidly moving river during a storm and got swept downstream to drown. Accidents will happen.

The following day, a beautiful 18-year-old named Jen, a product of Black-Asian parents and recent immigrant, fell ill with severe stomach cramps. She had a reputation for offering innovative programs in the underground gym.

"Honey, things occur in clusters," Carter said, late one night in the privacy of their personal campfire.

"They're all unrelated, aren't they?" she asked.

"Maybe a couple are unrelated, a half-dozen raises a red flag in my mind," he replied. Moment later he began a vomiting session that lasted for several hours. He split his time between the house and the bathroom. The next day another man wandered into the forest and never returned.

Carter awoke in pain well after sunrise to find Jess had gone. Dehydrated, he drank his fill, thinking nothing of it and having no appetite. Skipping breakfast, he began a cleaning stint at the turkey farm when he remembered Jess had wanted him to help her with some repairs to the house. He returned to find her absent and nowhere to be found. He called at the medical center and asked around to find that the last anyone had seen her was at breakfast.

He became seriously concerned when Carla could not be located either.

"Did she have an accident? Was foul play involved?" His mind reeled with dark thoughts, a normal process for a person concerned for a lost loved one. What didn't work was: "I'm sure she's fine. She can take care of herself."

4

Jess had never been this far into the Coconino forest, either alone or with company. A full hour out of the compound, she and Carla continued forward toward a beckoning range of red-orange hills that enraptured her. Occasionally, she would pause to critically examine some element of local flora, trying her skills at identification.

The appearance of occasional mule deer and wild turkeys excited Carla, who was ordered to stay. She did not receive rebuke when she caught and ate rabbits at will, something not a normal part of her directives. This served to confuse her. She might have wondered about it, if she had the capacity for wonderment. Rivulets and small streams offered cold, fresh liquid to the wanderers.

Another hour passed before she reached the rocks she sought. Their distance had fooled her; first near, then far, then near, their colors mesmerizing. The pair climbed to 300 feet where she found a flat rock to sit upon exposing her to the constant wind. She twisted her hat backward to protect her neck from the cold, while Carla seemed untroubled, satisfied to be next to her master.

The smell of smoke that she noticed when she first got up had diminished somewhat, possibly because the surrounding vegetation absorbed some of the odors. When she reached the outcropping of rock she looked to the north to see the unmistakable signs of a forest fire in the far distance, a not unusual event when frequent lightning strikes hit the large forest. The plume of smoke covered a broad swath of the horizon with the towering plume pointed in their direction, encouraged by the strong northerly winds.

Given enough time without rainfall at the area of the fire, it might well reach them in a few days, driving wildlife before it, engulfing the compound and forcing them to evacuate to a location yet to be described. At present, no escape plan existed for the community. Jess had nightmares about witnessing just such a scene, waking up to find every forest creature running through their community. Whatever the animals were running from, they'd better follow suit.

Looking back toward the direction from which she had come, Jess could see the ring of red rocks surrounding the compound. The poet in her took its charge. *This is your walkabout to define some destiny, to become secure in yourself, to strengthen faith.* Despite her self-reassurances, she felt terribly hollow, alone, and unfulfilled.

An instant later, in a flip-flop, Jess probed herself in a way she had never imagined could happen,
scanning her own body, searching her mind, trying
to assimilate the myriad of colors that ebbed and
flowed throughout her reverie that began several
minutes after breakfast. At times she felt as though
she were floating above the earth, her senses height-
ened in a way she had never encountered, totally enraptured by the life around her, feeling strangely one
with it all, from trees to insects to the rivulets that
sang crystalline tunes as they flowed over rocks.

"Time to move on, my dear. We'll keep going,"
she announced. Whenever Jess sat, Carla followed
suit. Whenever Jess stood to go anywhere, Carla
walked by her side unless instructed otherwise.

Above the tree line, she had a clear view of the
scudding clouds to the south, most of which presented faces of animals and people to her. She descended
from her perch and headed in the direction the sun
would set.

Back in the forest, Carla suddenly froze in place
and growled, causing Jess to stop, her own senses
alert. Before them stood a full-grown huge grey Si-
berian wolf from which Carla, and likely, all dogs,
had descended.

In dog terms, this presented a different case
where the sniffing of scent glands did not enter into
the picture. No mating in the offing here. Carla considered Jess her master, one she had to protect at all
costs. It had nothing to do with ancestry.

The wolf issued a hungry warning, signifying

winner take all.

Before Jess could pull the weapon from its holster in her rear waistband, the dogs charged one another. *Let them be,* she thought, trying to identify with Carla. Perhaps they both needed a good fight.

The two sider dogs met head-on, snarling, faster, stronger, and smarter than dogs of old, each going for a crippling move. To Jess, the fight appeared in slow motion. Each second's action was composed of 100 flip cards released one at a time, like a high-speed camera releasing images frame-by-frame. Blood soon appeared, from which animal Jess could not discern. She had no possibility of shooting the wolf with any certainty. This had become her personal fight.

In her own way, Carla was part human because of her understanding of human vocabulary and the intent behind the words, having grown up in a human world. Her animal instincts, integrating with her loyalty to her human masters, Jess in particular, gave her a ferocious quality reminiscent of prehistoric times when every waking minute meant a possible fight to the death. It gave her the edge she needed. She knew the taste of death.

The dogs disengaged and circled. Ready to fire a round into the wolf, Jess felt a reluctance to do so, to permit the scene to play out. She lowered her weapon. She and Carla were so bonded emotionally, if not psychically, they might as well have shared the same blood. Each protected the other. She let the fight continue.

After a dog fight that lasted for minutes too long, the wolf whined in dog-speak. In a moment, it turned and limped back into the forest, torn front and back, one ear shorn off. Carla did not pursue, gashed and tattered herself.

Jess came to her. "Stay here, I'll be right back to take care of you," she commanded, running to a nearby stream where she tore off a sleeve from her shirt and soaked it. In an instant she returned to apply it to Carla's numerous wounds ranging from the back of her neck to her haunches to a gash on above her right front leg.

Jess spoke soothing words, not cooing nonsense. There were words a six year old would understand, about love and caring and how they belonged together. Exhausted from the ordeal, woman and dog dozed until the sound of a distant gunshot awoke them.

Awakened by the sound, human and animal became alert. To Jess, she became confused by the merging of browns, greens, and blues surrounding her. Disoriented, she quickly headed off into the darkening forest without direction. After some time, she heard another gunshot, more distant from the first. She knew it for what it was: Someone might be trying to kill them. Paranoia forced her to walk faster, away from the sound behind her.

Search parties could find no sign of Jess or Carla in either section of the compound. Carter tried ringing the bell, calling for an emergency gathering of the populace, only to gain no information at all regarding her last whereabouts.

At last, Carter thought to engage Jay and for him to bring Riki, in the hope that the scent of Jess or Carla could be detected. Enthusiastically, Carla's brother followed instructions, found the scent of both woman and dog, and began to lead them into the forest. Hoping for the best, but prepared for the worst, Carter stayed the dog to take a few moments to gather water, medical supplies, a blanket, binoculars, and a sat phone The men followed the dog deep into the forest. Jay sent off a shot, hoping to hear return fire. He tried a second shot later to no avail. There would be no radio contact. She had left her radio at home. Another flash storm threatened to wash out any scents for Riki to follow.

Pausing at a small clearing, Jay scanned the only land-based area visible to the binoculars, the red rocks of a low hillock in the distance. Seeing no sign of the pair, the men began a rapid jog with Riki in the lead. Taking brief rest stops, the men continued to follow Riki. Finally, he began barking and raced forward, hearing Carla bark in return. In a few moments, men caught up with Jess. Surprised to see them, she caroled, "Oh, hi honey, Jay. What are you doing here?"

Carter, relieved at seeing her, couldn't stop his mouth. "We tried to signal you. Didn't you hear us? Why didn't you signal us back? Why didn't you take a radio?"

Jay interrupted the interrogation and said, "Look

at her eyes. They're glazed."

Jess stared through her husband without uttering another sound, while Riki began to lick Carla's wounds. Carter pulled out his sat phone and told Ken that in another mile they should reach a road where he can meet them. Wrapping the blanket around her, the five made their way to the dirt road that curved around the section leading to a long overgrown tourist site where all they joys of nature could be appreciated.

5

Carter forced Jess to drink copious amounts of water over the next 24 hours to flush out the toxins from her body. He did the same. Both had been poisoned, but not as badly as many others.. Both were dehydrated. The water immersion technique helped somewhat, and still somewhat giddy, Jess felt compelled to meet with the doctors on serious business two days later.

The medical center smelled of an overuse of chlorine bleach and vinegar. Smoke blowing down from the raging and rapidly approaching fire to the north could be smelled indoors. Hanging art that once adorned the walls of UL-One now adorned those of the room. Jess sat in the reception area with Carla lying at her side, comfortable in a familiar setting. In the background, a constant wind passed through the conifers to serve as a background moan, a default setting, like a mother constantly humming sing-song to her children.

Jess scratched Carla's ears almost absently, struggling to frame the right questions. She finally decided to take the neutral approach, considering herself capable of separating fact from fantasy. "Help me understand. What do we know? I'd like to have your opinions." She trusted these life-long friends.

Danny sat in a folding chair opposite her. The young woman needed to understand the variables. She might have become a good doctor, had she chosen that route. Considering her young age, she might be recruited yet. "Jess, we think they're random events so I wouldn't make too much of it. Insects are not the cause of the problem because the symptoms are so varied. Any stomach contents we examined show no abnormal food substances." At that point, he went into teaching mode to one who had been UL-One's best science student and explained what made sense and what didn't.

Jess didn't like what she heard, which basically amounted to nothing. After several minutes, Alex added, "You need to understand that, in all honesty, we are not toxicologists and lack the instruments, tools, and background to conduct a more in-depth investigation."

Jess knew this much. "Given what you say is true, what theories do you have, however fanciful they might be?"

Danny replied, "I explained to you about Blondie. As for the others, we agree with Carter. We have a cluster of events without a single common bond. Actually, I see two possible bonds, one physical and one mental, as exemplified by Carter's recent bout of stomach issues and your recent loss of reality. We could easily fit the other occurrences into those two groups. I see those as low-dose reactions. In other words, it could have been much worse."

It was no secret that the doctors lacked experience in autopsies; in fact, Alex had never performed one and Danny's single experience went back over 30 years to medical school. What Carter did hold secret was that the doctors had done a Class A-1 job in carving up Blondie, trying to read and learn as they went, acknowledging they needed equipment and experience. Equipment included more scalpels, a variety of blunt tip scissors, bone saw, rib shears, absorbent materials, an adjustable height metal autopsy table, a good microscope, and some sort of recording device. Wet dripping gloves did not mesh well with picking up a pencil to write down their findings and impressions.

Although Carter loved his wife dearly, he felt no need to share with her the doctors' requests for tools they could use for autopsies. Once that happened, he knew she would revert to the human condition and would, forevermore, visualize Blondie, the women she had known all her life, as having been cut down the middle with her organs removed. He would do his best to avoid that.

In addition, the doctors would greatly appreciate a place where they could perform the beastly work, not a make-shift covered area as an add-on to a parking lot. Should the need arise again, they wanted to be better prepared.

It was as though two separate disease-causing agents had invaded their community to affect younger and older victims equally. If it they were transmitted via food, then mass poisoning would be present and the problem should be easy to solve. If someone were a carrier, well, absolutely every able-bodied person worked in food preparation, something that had always been a way of life. These days, people either foraged for wild edibles, worked some aspect of the greenhouses, assisted with meal planning and food preparation, or worked at serving or cleanup. It all operated like clockwork after many years of repetition. To find the carrier would be an impossible task.

Furthermore, if some people reacted to a particular food item, such as with an allergic reaction or intolerance of some kind, then the symptoms should be fairly similar among them. Everybody knew that. Some people were known to be sensitive to eggs, still others to tomatoes or cucumbers. Occasional mild to severe reactions would occur. Nothing new there.

Seeking minor respite for the tensions of the day, the family of five, all wearing windbreakers, strolled to the end of the river to check the net for trout. A heavy rainfall to the north appeared to have quenched the fire. The toddlers clung to Carla's long fur, walking slowly enough for them to maintain their grip.

Jess asked, "What do you think the doctors mean

there might be two types of symptoms? Or did I already ask you that?"

"Several times," Carter replied. "Here's my take. You and I were targeted."

Carter saw Jess struggling with Topsider vocabulary and idioms. She confessed, "Targeted means . . ."

Expecting this response, Carter said, "Somebody used us a target, they're playing with us, teasing us, giving us low doses of their poison, challenging us to find them."

Reaching the net, the couple saw that fish fairly boiled at its surface, trapped, waiting to be collected. Carter made a radio call to Jay who said he'd be right down.

Targeted. Carter became suffused with a malice that boiled of its own, a malice and anger he had shoved down a long time ago, but the bubble burst into an emotion he forced himself to own, as a part of himself: The desire to rip and tear totally without remorse. To him, open warfare had its extensions, which meant that if the nation were gone, the same rules applied: take care of business, eschew glory, have no regrets, move on. His emotions overcame his hard-earned self-discipline. He was so tired of playing black on the chess board, reacting to the every move the white piece made. It all boiled down to five words: Somebody will be very sorry.

As her protector, he needed to ensure his wife felt the same way for the sake of survival.

6

Carter had shown a piece of himself Jess didn't like, a piece he didn't want to talk about. When she tried to fit his feelings into herself, she immediately rejected them, in part because raw hatred was as foreign to her as the surface world once was. She had to wonder if she would learn to accept and compartmentalize these dark new emotions.

Annie and Brenda took seriously ill the day after Jess tried her best to calm Carter's rage. Danny explained, "After breakfast, Brenda said she began hallucinating. An hour later, Annie complained of symptoms similar to yours, Carter, but no hallucinations." *Two types of symptoms.*

Alex tilted his head his head to the rear, "Annie's in the bathroom throwing up. One of our nurses is with her. Brenda is here in the next room. It's not pretty."

"I'll wait here for Annie," Jess said. "You go."

Both doctors followed Carter into the room

where Brenda lay on the cot, hands gesticulating and mumbling incoherent sentences.

"What's she saying?" Carter asked.

Danny gave a brief shrug. "Nothing tangible. Everything from different end of world scenarios, to poisoned food, to siders trying to kill everyone here."

Carter didn't need to hear that. He took a step over to the table. "Brenda, this is Carter. Do you know who I am?"

Brenda focused her eyes on him for an instant and said, "Carter, I'm so happy you're here?" A moment later she began to gesticulate again.

Carter said, "What are you doing for her?"

Alex lamented, "There's nothing we can do. We gave her an oral sedative, but it hasn't taken effect yet. This is beyond anything we've encountered. And our citizens who specialized in abnormal behavior and the paranormal are buried under concrete." Lowering his voice, he leaned closer and confessed, "She thinks the paranormal is involved—you know, possession and that kind of thing."

Ignoring Alex's last statement, Carter said, adamantly, "We don't need that talk about siders getting out. You know better than I do about how superstitious your people are."

"Too late for that now, Danny said. "She was ranting about siders before Gregor hauled her in here. Then he found out that Annie got the sickness and brought her in afterward. A.J. is tending to another case in the residence hall."

"How can he help?" Carter inquired.

"Not much, directly," Alex answered. "Take case histories, temperatures, write notes. We need to keep files on medical incidents. I instructed him to give salt water to patients to induce vomiting. That should assist in the lessening the symptoms over time. In other words, it won't help now. It should help later."

"Are you seeing any psychosomatic cases involving identification with the ill?" Carter offered.

Alex replied, "Not yet, but we expect that to occur at some point. Frankly, we can't do more for them here than we can do for them at home."

Carter mumbled, "What a shit storm."

Recovering from his momentary expression of frustration, Carter scratched the back of his head, starting to wonder if he had lost it, and flipped into a total non sequitur by saying, "I think we found you a vet hospital."

The term "vet hospital" could be construed to be a misnomer. A few of the remaining buildings still standing in Sedona belonged to a small strip mall. One of them titled itself a veterinary hospital. The office consisted of a waiting room and appointment desk, small bathroom, doctor's private office, and exam area. No surgeries were performed other than the smallest types and it possessed no facilities for no overnight stays. Still, it would provide the medical staff the space they required to use a greater range of procedures than they were able to do currently.

Annie's health returned to normal after three days, although Brenda complained of occasional flashbacks and out-of-body experiences. Ken's wife Beth, and Annie, sat with the medical staff, which included the two doctors, and A.J., a doctor in training. Jess sat with them. Charles Bailey, long time attorney, sat with the group. He had integrated with the underground city a generation ago since its inception and assisted the council in various legal matters of dispute since his arrival. Like a Swiss Army Knife, attorneys held many useful tools, if and when you need one. Bailey did his best to ensure everyone knew of his availability.

They sat on opposite sides of the long table, like two teams ready to face off. Bailey sat at the end, his usual position as arbitrator. The man appeared fiftiesh, with a full head of black hair, large, dark eyes, childish face, and diminutive stature, yet confident, popular and overall good looking. As an avocation, he performed in the theater arts. Beth served as the lone outsider and the single person who had never been to UL-One; however, like Annie, she did play a major role in the preparation of daily meals.

After ruling out food allergies, Danny said, "The only chemical I know of that can cause these kinds of problems is the alkaloids in some mushrooms. By problems, I'm referring to upset stomach, diarrhea, and hallucinations. We have different symptoms in different people and there a several explanations for that."

Jess added, "From what I've read about psilocybin, it definitely can cause paranoia, psychotic episodes, inability to separate reality from fantasy, and a variety of other symptoms, including flashes of creative insight. We haven't seen any of the latter yet, but a lot of the former. I recently experienced many of these symptoms, as you know."

Annie contributed, "The only mushrooms we did grow here were the same simple white button *Agaricus* and the *Shitake* for protein, vitamins and antioxidants. So that's out." Her Russian accent served to emphasize the point.

Jess offered, "There are other possibilities of foods that have alkaloids. The most well-known is belladonna or deadly nightshade, and ergot that grows on rye. We don't have either of those here."

Danny said, "Different doses can cause a variety of symptoms in different people. Many times poisons can have curative effects. For example, belladonna was used to alleviate arthritis in low doses. Annie, why don't you check your plants for anything that might being growing that shouldn't be there?"

Annie's face reddened beneath her short graying hair. She was about to come back with a fiery retort, as though the doctor had accused her of murder, when Beth placed a staying hand on her arm and said, calmly, "We'll check it out."

"There may be another possibility," Jess suggested. "Insects."

"How so? Other than bite marks on Blondie, none of our patients reported getting bitten or stung," Alex stated.

Jess continued, "We know we have mutants and variants of everything The Mars Virus touched. We've seen stingers and greens and we know they're toxic, so why can't there be other smaller toxic insects that might be hard to see that get into our food supply or attack us directly, maybe not even leave a mark when they bite."

Annie had run out of patience. "You're suggesting we check every leaf and stem of every plant we have to look for insects we can't see. Is that right?"

Believing her own idea might have some merit, Jess replied, in her best scientific manner, "No, let's look for the ones we can see. If any are poisonous, it may not take many to cause harm, but at least we can try to rule it out. Other theories would be helpful."

Alex said, "Maybe there is a pest that's taking over, maybe it's a fungus of some sort. At least we have a couple of ideas to work on."

Beth first looked at Annie, who had not yet recovered from her perceived accusation, "All right. We'll instruct all of our shifts to begin a thorough investigation of both greenhouses and let you know the results."

"And what exactly do we do once we find them?" Annie queried.

Nobody had an answer.

Beth announced, "There's talk of siders being responsible for this problem."

At that moment, and always happy to throw in his expert opinion, Bailey said, "Be careful about accusing anybody."

"It was a simple statement, Chuck, not an accusation. Keep your nose out of it," Annie shot.

If two people could be opposites, Annie and Charles Bailey were like oil and water. If they were ever thrown together in a situation, they would never mix and would separate quickly. She had no problem telling people she had bad feelings about the man. Furthermore, she had no problem being called out for glaring him if they found themselves in the same eatery together down below. Life on the surface did nothing to change her attitude toward him. Jess had told her that hatred like hers could take years off one's life. Upon hearing those words, Annie announced that, without a shred of doubt, intense hatred can be transmitted to another person to cause them to have bad luck, science be damned.

For his part, Bailey did not need Annie's Russian-accented lip, something he had put up with for too long. Doubtless, jealousy played a role in her attitude toward him. Robert, Jess's father and long-term mayor of UL-One, was a different story. The two were the closest of friends and Robert frequently permitted Bailey to attend council meetings, following his advice on legal matters and sharing meals together. Even Brenda Russo, the new mayor, continued to follow in Robert's footsteps, frequently calling him "sir" during the meetings. Both gave him the respect he deserved, a respect still retained by virtually everyone to this day. Being ignored was one thing he would not tolerate.

Beth suggested, "Let's keep our concerned citizens so busy looking for bugs they won't have time to get involved in idle gossip. After all, isn't gossip the playground for those who have no other way to play?"

"True," answered Jess, "Unfortunately, superstition and gossip go hand-in-hand, which may be our greatest concern, one that could tear apart our community."

Once the meeting adjourned, Beth approached Annie and asked, "I finally saw this Bailey guy people talk about. What's his deal?"

Annie snorted. "He's one of the older members of the refugees. According to him, he used to be a prosecuting attorney then switched to defense, said he made ten times the money defending gangsters. Whenever there was anything that even smelled legal down below, he'd be there front and center. I guess he tries to compensate for his height, or lack of it. Personally, I never believed a single word of it. Too self-confident for me. A real pain." Once she had completed her rudimentary survey of the man, Annie went to provide Beth with a more profound subjective opinion of him firmly believing the bad vibes would go straight to Bailey's heart.

Bailey had people convinced he was almost priest-like, in that, even though they were not his clients, in his humble opinion, attorney-client privilege still pertained. Therefore, their deepest secrets would be safe with him. Superficially, Charles Bailey appeared sociable, chatty, informative, and companionable, until one dug a little deeper when the truism came to the fore: Unfettered self-confidence can lead to arrogance. Self-confidence, in its turn, can be based on false narratives. Charles Bailey possessed a combination of the three, all of which ran deeply enough to be unattractive qualities the deeper one delved. Therefore, unless legal advice was sought, it might be best not to dig too deeply because the well could prove to be shallow and dry.

He did know a lot about a lot of people. Also, although younger than Bailey by a good quarter century, Jess did serve as the mayor of her own city. It made sense to be friendly with her, in case she needed to share any of her own secrets. There existed a certain exploitable naiveté about the woman.

7

A group of seven men and women stood around the school bus watching Ken pull a plug from the engine. He inspected the carbon load and checked the gap by sliding in a gauge. He cleaned off the carbon, adjusted the gap and returned the plug to the engine. He passed the socket wrench to the next person who would do the same with the next plug in line. Then he pulled the dip stick from the engine, wiped it off, reinserted it, pulled it out again and checked the oil level, instructing the others to do the same and to check the other fluids.

During the process, Gregor came running over in their direction, saw the group and yelled, "Don't even think about it, I'm armed." He got into a white long-bed van they had refurbished, and sped away. Seconds later Carter came running. "He's whacked," Carter said.

Ken replied, "He said he's armed. Did you see his gun?"

"No, but we better see if we can catch him," Carter said, out of breath, as he climbed into his truck.

Ken directed his class, "Keep working." He jumped into the passenger seat and Carter sped off after Gregor.

Gregor's van was no match for Carter's big V-8. Tried and tested over years on the roads between the compound and Sedona proper, he knew every pothole and obstruction and soon gained on the van. He could see Gregor checking his driver's side mirror to see how close they were before trying to go faster, a reckless and foolhardy move on the three mile stretch of road, with every chance of destroying both man and car.

Ken directed, "If you pull parallel with him and he's armed, he may shoot. Get on his right side and I'll get in the back seat behind you and take a shot at a tire."

Within seconds Carter had faked left to draw Gregor to pull left, then swerved right and punched it. At this point they could only drive at relatively low speeds in the pitted roadway, which forced Gregor to slow on occasion. Both men always wore side-arms and Ken leaned out the window slightly and fired two rounds, one of which hit the van's right rear tire. Carter backed off immediately to watch the van slow considerably, then go off the road and stop in a shallow ditch.

Both men cautiously exited the truck. "Get out, Gregor," Ken yelled.

"I'm not getting out, you can't have me," Gregor

yelled.

Ken motioned to Carter who nodded. Ken went to the driver's side and Carter to the passenger's side of the van. With guns drawn, both men yanked open the doors at the same time. Gregor, confused, confronted Ken who grabbed him by the left arm and yanked him hard out of the truck. Somehow, Gregor maintained his balance, and swung wide at Ken who ducked and rammed his own fist deep into the other man's mid-section. At the same instant, Carter came around and kicked Gregor's knees from behind to drop the man. Fortunately, he did not have a weapon, but his paranoia led him to believe he did. He lay on the ground with muscle spasms, in full fear of anybody around him, and there was little anybody could do about it until it wore off, which could take days.

8

Although no untoward event occurred over the next week, meal preparation became a challenge. People ate less, skipped a meal, or ate only selected items at their preference, fearful of the unknown lurking in the food. When they did chance a meal, odds against getting poisoned were not good. The entire community suffered from fear, which became the primary topic of conversation. Members of the council were not excluded from this paranoia, as three members had already been affected.

It is almost forbidden for there to be an excessive amount of leftover food, so the serving staff and those willing to eat more were invited to return after mealtimes had concluded to finish off any remains.

Although she wouldn't complain, Jess still suffered from headaches. Gregor, Brenda and Annie recovered completely, as did a few minor cases attended to by the medical staff. Working almost as obsessive-compulsive robots, anyone working in the greenhouses did their share to ensure no insects of note were present and no plants had an unaccountable infection.

However, Annie complained to Jess that people were beginning to steal from the greenhouses during their shift. "We collect a certain number of items for each meal and put them in a tub prior to preparation. I think workers are stealing from the tub. They'd rather eat it fresh than take a chance of eating a meal after it has gone through several hands. Honestly, I can't blame them."

"Do you think it might be a bad strain of something causing the problems" Jess asked innocently, fingering aeroponically grown bean sprouts that had overgrown their basket to hang down in a large cluster to form a green inverted cone.

"Not a chance. I've eaten everything here on my own and I feel fine," she reported.

Jess scratched her neck, looking up at the polypropylene covering over the greenhouse and the tiers of colorful fruits and vegetables maturing more rapidly due to the infection by the virus, as did all vegetation. "If somebody is poisoning us, couldn't it be on the food line? Instead of rotating our staff, what if we maintained the same servers, ones we trust. See if the poisonings stop."

Annie shrugged, "That's a good idea. By the way, you know there's talk about people voting in a new council, or at least, a new mayor."

Jess felt deflated. As mayor, she should be privy to gossip, yet she only had herself to blame by not mingling more with the citizens. Instead, she spent too much time in the medical center, reading, and playing with her children. The mayoral position did not satisfy her to any depth and she reconsidered turning over the position to someone more enthusiastic about being a politician. She was an academician who only wanted to search the depths of science.

Jess paced back and forth. "Back up, Annie, we've been doing this every day for over 20 years. Say somebody is poisoning the food on their rotation. What are the possibilities? We've got food pickers, cleaners, preparers, servers, and dish washers. People line up and get a plate or a bowl. Two dishes maximum. Okay, plus silverware. They eat, put their used dishes and silverware in the respective container. They're immediately washed, dried, and stacked, ready for the next shift. If we lock people into certain tasks and the poisonings stop, it doesn't necessarily mean anything. You can't add poison to a dish you washed, can you? My brain is starting to melt."

"It's not in my greenhouses, plain talk," Annie said. "Beth and I oversee them like hawks circling in search of moving prey. We'll go with your idea of locking in three people as servers. You pick up a bowl, get a couple of ladles of stew or soup of the day, a piece of bread, and some dessert. Or you pick up a plate for meat, potatoes and vegetables. You hand it to server who doles it out, move to the next server, and you sit down. Same two or three servers.

All other rotations stay the same."

Once the changes were instituted, the poisonings continued at the rate of one or two per week, although an occasional week or two would pass without incident. The doctors strongly suspected psychosomatic complaints by identification with the symptoms, as Carter had suggested earlier.

Jess had no answers. She felt as though she were a babe lost in the land of giants, not only in terms of size, but in terms of overwhelming problems. Either she needed more information, or perhaps she might be looking at the problem the wrong way.

The temperature had warmed to the mid-60s. As resident meteorologist, Jess always watched for a rapid change in wind direction which usually preceded the appearance of black thunderheads at the northern or northwestern horizon. Late one morning, soon after ringing the storm warning bell, two citizens reported ill with the same symptoms that had wrought fear in the community not long before. Both died within hours. Loading the deceased into the van, Ken and Gregor followed Danny and Alex, who drove Beth's SUV, to the veterinary hospital in Sedona to perform their work, sans adequate tools.

Despite the warning bells, knots of people began to form in the streets, giving Jay sidewise glances while he came from the river to speak with Jess, who still stood by the bells outside their home. "Greetings, Mrs. Mayor," he intoned.

"Not such a fine morning, I'm afraid. They're

talking about siders," she intoned.

Jay laughed. "Those darn siders. They're the root of all evil. Anyway, I came over to ask if you know where I can get some metal strapping like they used on old barrels without us having to go into town. Wei and I need some to reinforce our fish screens."

Jess thought a moment and replied, "I'd check in the old barn next to the Big House where we got the two ATVs. I thought I saw some barrels in the camera feed when the drone first scanned the place."

"Good idea. How much time do we have before the storm hits? An hour?"

"At the most," she said. "I'll go with you. We'll grab one of those ATVs."

"All right. Let me get a pair of cutting shears in case we find something." Jay departed for a moment.

Shortly, the couple drove the road to the Big House, crossed the bridge, and pulled up at the entrance of the barn next to the house. Walking inside, "I think I saw them in the corner over there when the drone came in," Jess said, leading the way to where four empty oak barrels stood, each some 30 inches in height.

Jay began snipping, while Jess looked around and upward. In a matter of seconds, he had snipped three six-foot long metal straps bordering two of them. He laid them out and began to gather them in a pile to take to the ATV when Jess asked, "What do you think is up in the loft? From here it looks like a pile of old suitcases and boxes."

Jay looked up said, "Let's find out."

He set down the strips and the two climbed the wooden ladder to find stacks of dusty suitcases, cardboard boxes, and clothing trunks. Walking over to the pile Jay looked over them. A moment later he called, "Jess, look at this."

Immediately at his side, she peered over his shoulder. They began to slide away boxes to find a two-burner hotplate with a number of pots and glass jars stacked against the wall behind it. Jay announced, "Mason jars and screw caps, picking up one of a dozen filled with liquid.

Jess took it from his hand, almost dropping it when she saw what it contained. She set it down gently as though it were filled with nitroglycerin. "Jay, it's an *Aminitas muscaris* mushroom. "

"I'm not a mushroom kind of guy. Help me out here?" Jay requested.

Jess gathered herself She held up the jar, instructing, "This is classic. It's a bright red mushroom with white spots on the cap. The genus grows in association with pines and other trees, sharing nutrients and sugars, symbiotic, you know. It is psychoactive. Somebody here is very smart."

"How do you know this?" Jay asked, looking at his junior of more than 20 years with a new respect.

"I don't know. I read a lot, I guess," she replied, picking up another jar, wondering where, in fact, she had gleaned the knowledge. A moment later she inserted, "I guess, because I have a book called *Edible and Inedible Plants of the Coconino Forest*. It also has pictures and descriptions."

Picking up another jar, she announced, "*Psilocybe* or death cap. The combination of the two will seriously affect the central nervous system including the brain, cause a reduction in red blood cell count, and destroy the kidneys. The short version is they're both deadly and hallucinogenic."

"Or can probably cause a variety of clinical conditions in lower doses, I would surmise?" Jay added.

"Correct. It would also depend on the person, the species, what's already in their stomach--a host of variables," she instructed, fascinated by the collection she saw before her, all the more impressed by other jars containing toxic species without being psychoactive. Many of them appeared completely harmless.

"You don't learn this stuff overnight. This takes planning and foreknowledge," she offered, totally overwhelmed by the magnitude of the finding.

"You know your people. Who is capable of doing this?" Jay needed answers. This business of poisoning and killing had to end. His genius as applied to the fields of biochemistry and engineering were renown, yet he had no idea how to ferret out the perpetrator(s) of these horrific events. Nobody did.

Jess replied, "In all honesty, our educational system was so intense anyone could have collected these, although we never saw them. Cooking them properly to extract their toxic agents takes practiced skill."

Jay said, "Won't the boiling process destroy the toxic agent?" He had no problem deferring to one more knowledgeable.

"Yes, in a lot of cases. Some toxins survive boiling water, most can be extracted well before the water gets to that point," Jess answered, opening and looking into small cardboard boxes as she spoke.

"Whoa, look here," she declared, reaching into one to pull out a small mortar and pestle set constructed of ceramic. A thin crust of off-white powdery substance coated the bottom of the pestle and the bottom of the mortar. "Somebody has been grinding something and I think I know what it is."

First, putting her nose close to the mortar, she waved her hand over it, trying to create a waft of musty air to enter her nose. Then, touching her index finger lightly to the bottom of the pestle, she touched the tip of her tongue to the substance on her finger and said, "Liquid and solid. It looks as though somebody has two methods of delivering poison. Ingenious. Nothing like making sure the job gets done."

9

Jay held up one of the glass jars containing a red-capped mushroom completely immersed in liquid, including its stem. "Is the psilocybin in the stem or the cap of the mushroom?" he inquired.

"Both cap and stem have active agents. The cap has the highest concentration," she reported, taking the jar from Jay's hands, holding it up to get a better view.

Jay exhaled, resignedly, and announced, "Let's put things back the way they were and see if we can find out who's doing this. I'll ask Wei to fly the drone in here and park it, say, downstairs, on one of the hay bales and leave the camera on. The battery will last a long time as long as the motor isn't running. We can watch the monitor to see who comes in."

"Let me check out something," Jay added. He followed the power cord from the burner and found it connected outside to the grid associated with the waterwheel. "Somebody knows the basics," he muttered.

"Like I say, could be any one of our people, including you and me," she answered.

Returning the jars and boxes to their original position and preparing to climb down the ladder, Jess said, "Wait, what are those three really big boxes against the wall. I couldn't see those from the ground."

Jay said, "Those are called trunks. People used to store clothing in them for travelling on long journeys, or for storage at home."

"Really, clothing? I want to see," she said, excitedly. She had a sudden vision of finding a colorful shawl or something comfortable she could wear around the house. Fingering a padlock, she added, "Let's open one."

Anxious to report the mini-chemistry lab they had discovered, Jay acceded to her wishes, climbed down the ladder and returned a moment later with an iron bar. In seconds he had broken the lock and removed it. "You can have the honors," he offered, trying not to disturb the thick layer of dust that covered the top.

Cautiously, Jess open the trunk and both of them stared at the contents. "What am I looking at?"

Jay did not reply.

"Jay?" she repeated.

Jay tried his best to remain objective when he said, "I wouldn't expect you to know what any of that is. On the left is bound stacks of $100 bills. It's what used to be money printed by the United States. I'm guessing the big packages on the right wrapped in plastic are cocaine."

"I don't get it," she shook her head, clearly mystified.

Jay chuckled and took a few minutes to explain to her the drug-running business, after which she asked, "Do you think that's why there was a shootout at the Big House before we first discovered it?"

Jay said, "Could be a lot of reasons. Could have been a simple break-in attempt. Let's see what's in the other two. Maybe you'll get lucky and find some clothes you like."

The second trunk was similar to the first except the money consisted entirely of $5s, $10s, $20s, and 50s, all looking worn and used.

Money occupied the third trunk.

Jay replaced the broken padlocks and took a last look around to ensure everything was as they found it, sans broken locks, and the couple climbed down the ladder. Jay picked up his lengths of strapping and the pair returned to the compound with the smell of incoming rain to greet them.

The almost continuous wind had increased its intensity and the first heavy drops forced the knots of gossipers to disperse. Jay went straight to Wei and Jess found Carter closing the hood of his dually. A buzzing sound caused them to turn their attention. The drone had taken flight above the boulders heading toward the river where it would fly low, staying out of the wind on its way to the barn.

Jess summoned the council members to a meeting. She also invited Gregor, because one of his primary duties in the homestead was to work security and this definitely fit into that category. Jess recounted what she and Jay had discovered in terms of the mushroom cooking. She informed the members about the contents of the trunks and they stipulated to focus on the issue of poisonings for this discussion.

Gregor said, "How would they do it on an individual basis? If the poison is added to the food in a solution, everybody would get sick, not one or two at a time. So they're not putting it in one of the big vegetable or meat pots."

Wei offered, "If I wanted to do something like this, I would have to be on the food serving line and have a little container of the stuff, which I would pull out and slip the contents into somebody's individual portion. Maybe even two or more small containers, one for each person—something easily concealed."

Ken asked, "Why certain people and not others? It seems almost random. Everybody works on the serving line in their turn. It could be absolutely anyone here."

"Maybe the person doesn't care who they poison or kill. It's the thrill of power, of watching us run around in fear," Carter added, all too readily recalling his own sickness and others he considered part of his family: Jess, Annie, and Gregor.

"My first thought is of Brenda, but she wouldn't

poison herself," Jess said. After a moment of silence, she chimed, "Or would she?"

Annie said, "Here's a theory for what it's worth. A lot of us here have known her for many years. She has a history of alcohol and *Cannabis* abuse. No big deal unto itself. Add the fact she's outspoken and likes to take charge, and served as mayor of our city."

"Come on, Annie, admit you don't like her," Jess said.

"No, I don't," Annie snapped. "Now hear me out. Suppose she found a new vice and takes it in small enough doses to give her a sense of well-being, except some of this stuff is psychoactive and can bring about hallucinations. Suppose she overdosed one day, say the same time she poisoned me, and we both wound up in the medical center. "

Jess said, "Good analysis. Seriously, except for Jay, she knows more organic and biochemistry than anybody here thanks to her family's history in the wine business. At one time, she had asked me if I wanted to work with her to develop a cleaner alcohol."

"And, she does live at the Big House," Gregor inserted.

"And, I'm the one who put her there," moaned Ken.

Carter warned, "Be careful, guys. It's a perfect case for circumstantial evidence without proof. It's called a witch hunt. You're turning somebody into a witch who fits your definition of a witch. There are another ten living in that house, or it could be some-one here who goes out at night and works alone, or even with a partner."

Annie laughed. "You sound like Bailey, now."

Carter ignored her. "We'll play the waiting game. Take shifts looking at the monitor and see what the doctors have to say."

"It could be a long wait," said Wei. "These events are spread apart and now we have two people going down today. We're getting whittled down to, what, 130 or so along with two grown dogs and six wolf not-so-small pups?"

Jess contributed, her mind remembering and computing. "The poison still has to be brewed and tended to, unless they have a stash. Plus, it looks like there are at least two classes of toxins at work here, one is psychoactive and the other is more poisonous. The stash part scares me. Heck, it's easy enough to make. If it were me, I'd use a little alcohol as a non-polar solvent to enhance the extraction. Either way, it gets into the bloodstream, eats at the kidneys and liver and settles into the myelin sheath surrounding the central nervous system."

"If there is a stash of sufficient size, it could be enough to kill everyone in a single day," Wei said, without emotion, letting the enormity of her statement to sink in.

"Nasty stuff. Where's Brenda now?" asked Ken.

"Helping with cleanup, I think," Beth replied.

"Let us know when she heads for home," Carter requested.

"There is a second matter for discussion, which you have all been briefed on," Jess stated. "Carter, you went up there. What do you think?'

"Between the coke and the money, there's millions up there. I don't know a use for either of them," he answered.

Ken stated, "I say hang on to the money. It's not hurting anything and it might become useful someday, if only to light a fire with."

"No big deal there," Jay said. "The cocaine is another matter. Maybe the doctors can find something to do with it."

Jess said, "Jay's got a point. Maybe they can use it as a painkiller."

"Twenty kilos of the stuff?" Carter asked.

"Do you think the mushroom chef in the loft knew about the trunks?" Gregor asked, innocently.

"Probably not," Ken said. "Think it through. Makes no sense. They were padlocked and he or she would need a key. Where would they get the key? It wouldn't be hanging on a hook by the front door of the house. Anyway, reportedly, the bags were intact. Three containers of stored potential energy in another life, basically useless today."

Several hours later, Brenda took the walk back to the Big House, but the monitor showed no activity in the barn. Danny called and reported that he and Alex wouldn't return back from their dissections until the early morning hours and he'd be in contact after they got some sleep. At night, various members of the group took shifts keeping a wary eye on the screen.

10

"Inflammation of the brain meninges, irritation of the linings of the stomach and small intestine. Unfortunately we don't have a microscope to do RBC counts. It's consistent with ergot poisoning and what you found in the loft," Alex reported, throwing down the file folder on the table. His father had decided to sleep in after the long night.

Ken picked it up, looked at the reports and passed the folders to Carter, who did the same, then passed the reports to Gregor.

Ken laughed, "I guess we're getting nowhere fast."

Carter suggested, "All we can do is keep a vigilant eye out and keep it to ourselves so we don't scare away the bad guy." He paused, thought a moment, and added, "On the other hand, we could force their hand by making a general announcement. We can say we're looking at making even more improvements to our housing and list a few that would seem normal and ask for suggestions. Among them, we might casually mention the barn and we're looking into renovating it to make living quarters.

"In terms of practicality, it can't be done. There is no way to get enough materials and workers out there coming and going to accomplish the job; I mean the bridge isn't strong enough or large enough to support a heavy vehicle carrying a load of passengers and supplies, but they don't have to know that. Way back, when they built the house, they must have come in from a different direction. If our criminal suspects our plan, they'd have to know their secret will be out once their little cooking venture gets discovered."

"Then we might not know who it is," said Ken.

"Yeah, that's the problem with my idea. Let's hope their lust for power overcomes their reluctance to fade into the woodwork," Carter concluded.

Carter informed Alex of the cocaine discovery. Ignorant of its history, Alex said he would defer the final decision to his father. After hearing about the find, Danny chose to keep the packages. With a small portion of it in their office, he might use it in terms of a poultice or in other matters where painkilling might be involved. Nobody needed to know. And if they did, so what? In their new world, UL-Oners still adhered to Gottlieb's dictum that only natural medications could be used. What could be more natural than a painkiller derived from cocoa leaves?

Several days of observation failed to reveal a single person entering the barn. Even a disguised marker Carter had hidden on the ladder remained undisturbed. Disgusted, he thought about bringing a trash bag to the loft to collect the cooking items, but decided to wait a few more days. As he did no, two more mild poisonings occurred during that interval, which brought angry citizens to Jess's door demanding she step down as mayor.

"And Mrs. Mayor," many asked, "where were Jay and Wei in all of this." She patiently explained that Carter had asked them to go to Flagstaff for a couple of weeks on a project, a reply met with scorn and suspicion. Conspiracy theorists announced that, instead of saber toothed tigers lurking in the tall grass ready to pounce, either the government or siders or both working in concert had taken their place. Jess argued that even members of the government had been poisoned, including her husband and Annie, not to mention Gregor, which, of course, fell on deaf ears because a cover-up knows no bounds.

Carter assessed the situation. "If this was three centuries ago, you and I would be burned at the stake. Conspiracies are an easy out. It makes life easier to cast blame on the most visible rather than the invisible. Whenever I come to a point of confusion, it tells me I don't have enough information. How do I get more information? For us, maybe we're looking in the wrong place. Maybe they've moved the setup to someplace else."

Jess's eyes lit up. A broad grin crossed her face. Giving him a quick kiss she said, "That's why I love you."

The detective in her led Jess to formulate a theory. She'd read too many crime novels to believe the perpetrator would feel remorse and suddenly quit their obsession. No, the feeling of power was a disease that became the master. Which meant someone must continue making their product, not just be satisfied with a stash, which meant there must be a secret location. She could think of a number of possibilities, and they all revolved around the caves—a full dozen of them on both sides of the river where the cavers had lived. One path leading to them began near the rear of their compound behind her home. A walk through the forest led to a short path downward to a ledge above a branch of the river where the caves were located. But someone traversing that path too frequently might arouse suspicion.

The other way to the caves was the road which led to the long and sometimes muddy climb down the hill to the nearest ledge. That would be the last way someone would chose to get there. She had never followed the ledge to the end. Apparently it led to some escape route the surviving cavers had taken to avoid the onslaught of Carter, Ken, and Gregor. It would be a long way for someone to come in from the far end; not impossible, but impractical.

However, the Big House lay up the hill only a couple hundred yards above the river's branch and the ledges. This suggested one of the caves might be housing the cooking items necessary for preparation of the poison. You really didn't need electricity or a hotplate. The high heat might speed up the cooking process, but nothing like a can or two of Sterno to do the job for a nice slow cook.

After mentioning her deductions to Carter, he thought for a second, then said, "Ken and I will take the path from here and begin with those on the near side and work our way to the smaller ones farther away. If your theory is right, they'll want a cave nearest the Big House and farthest from us. The last one is too small to call a home. It is big enough for a simple activity like heating a pot and storing some glassware containers."

Later that day, Carter reported, "Good call, sweetheart. There's a bridge cross the river right near that distant cave and more of them across the river. The good news is there's one directly opposite the one with the stove and you can't see into it. I'll ask Gregor if he wants to hole up there to see who shows up to do the cooking. Let's ask Bailey to spell him. He's always sticking his nose into things. Whoever reports it first gets a reward."

"What *do* we do if we see who it is? Capture them? Follow them?" Jess asked.

Carter pondered this. Neither Gregor nor Bailey were skilled at stealth. "Let them get away and report back to either me or Ken, and only us. We'll take care of it."

Jess knew her husband well enough to understand his meaning. The person could disappear and, hopefully, the poisonings would stop.

Reluctant to spend hours on end in a cave, but anxious to get into Jess's good graces, Bailey chose the second shift. The small cave had enough depth to eliminate the possibility of any person seeing him from across the river, even by accident. Reclining, he read from his slate each day until slightly before darkness fell, at which time he left for home while he could still see.

Growing weary of inactivity after six days, Bailey had begun to give serious thought about making this his last day and asking the powers to find someone else, when he saw movement. Pulling out the binoculars, he could easily see the cook stove in the cave across from where he hid. A person came from the left. He couldn't see whether he or she had come down the hill, or had taken the long path from the west.

The person wore baggy tan pants, long sleeve shirt, work boots, and baseball cap, all standard wear. Zooming in, he had no doubt Brenda had entered the cave. He watched her light the Sterno to heat water in the pot until steam arose. She then pulled a pouch from her belt and plucked out several red mushrooms which she put in the pot where she spent 20 minutes preparing the brew. She then pulled a ladle from somewhere and added the liquid to a large bottle then funneled the contents into several smaller bottles until reducing it further into perfume-size bottles. She also took the time to dry and grind several mushrooms to a powder, which she also saved. She placed collections of her incantations into her pouch, leaving the majority of the contents of her efforts by the stove. Then she extinguished the flame, put the lid back on the Sterno can, and left the cave.

With her back to him, Bailey could now go to the mouth of his own cave and watch her climb the hill some 20 yards away into the forest heading toward the Big House. He waited a few minutes to ensure she wouldn't return to recover some forgotten item, then he walked across the bridge. He entered the cave to inspect what he could of her work.

With one exception, everything looked the same as it was at their first discovery of the location. Mason and screw-cap jars of varying sizes stood against one wall, many with liquid in them to varying degrees. He picked up one of them and unclipped the top, dipped his finger into the liquid and tasted it to encounter the mustiness of mushroom scent. One of the four-ounce Masons contained ground pieces of mushroom, another had a number of small red mushrooms with white spots. He looked at the small cook stove and a number of empty and full jars nearby. A six-ounce screw cap with dented lid contained an off-white powder and another, next to it, a Mason of equal size, contained a liquid. A smaller clay mortar and pestle lay nearby

Bailey cautiously tasted both the powder and the liquid nearest the stove to encounter a slight bitterness. These were the ones she had drawn from before she left. These must be the poisonous varieties. He surmised some of the tan-looking mushrooms may contain differing amounts of active agents. He didn't know anything about mushrooms. He did find impressive the simplicity of her operation. Obviously, she didn't want to be caught with the bulk of the poison on her and she probably took what she could easily secret for her next round of activities. The realization provided him with an inspiration, a forbidden thought so delightful it caused blood to flow to his lower portions——an unauthorized salute from his nether parts.

Finding Jess, Carter, and Gregor seated together at dinner during the second shift, he joined them, nodding as he entered, then took a seat at an available spot to eat, thinking it likely he wouldn't be poisoned, at least not at the present meal. Brenda had not appeared. There was nothing unusual for a person to miss their meal shift for a variety of reasons, and occasional stragglers could be expected.

The four casually left the meeting hall, walking together to find a quiet spot out of the wind between the building and the boulders to speak. Parting company after several minutes, each went on their way. Carter found Ken, who had eaten earlier.

A person can be summoned to a meeting for a variety of reasons. Typically, Carla or Riki are sent to their great delight, to bark at their subject, grab at their pant leg, push them, or use other means to convey the message they are wanted and to follow them. Such was not the case with Brenda when she failed to appear at breakfast the following morning. The drone discovered her seated by the river throwing rocks in the water, oblivious of her hair flying in her face, her glazed eyes saw colors in the flowing water. This was fortunate for her pursuers who didn't want to confront her at home with witnesses present.

Two people came up behind her, unnoticed, until Carter spoke. "We found your cook stove and jars in the loft and then in the cave. You were being watched. Do you want to explain exactly what, why, and how you did it?"

Brenda's heart first jumped in surprise, then sank at his words, her eyes unfocused. Jess could feel the presence of darkness in front of them when she said, "Brenda, it's over. You're going to be expelled at best, if you tell us now what we want to know. If we turn this over to a committee of citizens, you will die. It won't be a pleasant death. Do one good thing."

Through tears that drew no sympathy, Brenda let it out, almost thankful to have the opportunity to end her own nightmare. "You know me, Jess. I guess I did it because I needed thrills in life. A new life on the surface offered those thrills, and also energized me in ways I couldn't control. At first I thought to have a little fun. The problem is, I couldn't control the dosages—people were supposed to get a little out of sorts and do odd things. I didn't mean for them to wander off and drown or die."

"Still, you kept doing it anyway," Carter added. "You poisoned me and my wife."

"I had to get the dosages right, don't you understand?" Brenda asserted, digging herself in deeper, not responding to the accusation.

"Tell us how you did it?" Jess prodded, her anger

mounting. The woman before them had become a twisted person. A victim of her own cultivation.

Brenda pulled herself into the real world long enough to explain that, prior to the desperate call from Danny about the collapse of the city, she observed Jay and Gregor leaving for Flagstaff to collect supplies. These included cosmetics at Beth's request. A variety of sizes of perfumes bottles were brought back, the contents of many were dated and degraded. These contents were discarded. Their glass containers, however, were washed out and saved.

Of these, she had chosen small flat wide-mouth types for faster pouring and secreted one or more of them in her waistband. She would pull one out while she speaking with the person in front of her for distraction, deftly unscrewing the cap with thumb and forefinger and then, like a magician palming a hidden object—in this case the open bottle—to pour it into the person's food. She practiced the maneuver several times and found she could accomplish the entire task within five seconds with the bottle recapped and restored into the waistband, where, perhaps, a second bottle might lay in wait.

Through it all, she found herself taking trace amounts of the psychedelics and occasionally overdosed. She confessed to having enjoyment in seeing she had never added anything to the food of several of those complaining of symptoms. Complaining can be a contagion unto itself. Even without her actions, the problem became self-perpetuating.

Only days later, people began to ask, "Where's Brenda?"

Jess explained, "We think a stinger got her and she wandered off. I want everybody to make sure to use plenty of bug oil. Somehow, she disappeared."

"She had a cushy job as maid over at the Big House. Who's going to take over?" many asked, not missing Brenda so much as seeing a good job opening.

"Oh, Charles Bailey helped us so much in the council that everybody agreed he should get the position."

One person remarked, "Good old insider politics works every time."

Another person sighed, "In a way I feel sorry for her," to which Carter replied, "Regarding Brenda, in my dictionary the word sympathy falls between shit and syphilis."

11

A week after Brenda's disappearance the poisonings began anew. The citizens began to yell for a new mayor. Because of his acting skills and sociability, Bailey suddenly found himself unofficially nominated for the position. No assistant mayor ever existed. He kept his dark side well hidden.

"This is the first time I've been interviewed for a job I didn't want," he complained. "Besides, I'm no leader."

"We need an interim mayor. Jess needs to step down," Ken said.

"Right, and all of a sudden the crime wave is going to stop with me as the fall guy," Bailey whined.

"It'll only be for a short while," Beth implored, looking at Jess, who nodded her ascent. Annie sat frozen staring daggers into the man, willing him to have a heart attack on the spot.

Bailey looked as though he were on the hot seat in a jury trial, instead of being offered the job as head of a township. Downcast for a moment, he gritted his teeth, looked up and said, "Look guys, I don't need this or want this. I'm a simple guy who likes to have fun."

Pausing for a moment, Bailey sat back in his chair and suggested, "Tell you what. I'll do it under two conditions: We do it for a month only and you take me off any kitchen duty. I hate kitchen work. Give me the greenhouse any day. Meanwhile, I'll go around and be nice to everyone and act mayoral, no offense, Jess."

"Three months?" offered Carter.

"Two months," returned Bailey.

"Done," proclaimed Jess, after looking around for approval.

Bailey first thought the offer by the city council would put him into a spotlight, one he didn't need for his overall game plan to work. An occasional performance in theater arts or sticking his nose into legal matters was not the same as being the center of attention all the time.

On second thought, underlying it all, he felt self-congratulatory. Everything might be falling into place. He may have walked into a gold mine. Everybody in their community knew about poisonous mushrooms and none had ever encountered them either grown hydroponically or aeroponically. Any mushrooms suspected of being other than the two varieties they used were culled out immediately. Historically, they'd been used for assassinations like any toxic substance humans could get their hands on. Mold growing on wet grain was long known to be a killer of horses, cattle, and humans. Until Brenda, he'd never thought of fungi being weaponized to terrorize a society.

When he had looked at Brenda's handiwork in the cave, he'd wondered what motivates a person to become an executioner and could come up with no answer. This led to the thought of power in the extreme. He tried wearing the feeling like a cloak and it thrilled him beyond anything he had ever experienced. It was better than holding a weapon people could see, which represented momentary respect, and like sex, it presented momentary pleasure.

Long-term good feelings were hard to come by. If you had the money or the means to change the world, how would you do it? The challenge of going undetected caused a surge of hormones to increase his heart rate and cause him to sweat. He could take her two prepared jars, collect a second non-toxic set to turn in, report her activities, and she'd be gone in a flash. Nobody would know. If the entire city believed food to be the culprit, so be it.

First, he needed to be in the clear and keep himself in plain sight without arousing suspicion, like a magician using a larger move to cover a smaller move. That meant staying away from kitchen duty altogether. Second, because he had no idea what dosage might be involved to cause a reaction, he could play a little, just to see what happened and go from there. Third, in order for it to work, he would have to come up with a new delivery system because he had no idea what hers had been. This would require a syringe. He thought he knew where he could get one. It might take a week or two, but anticipation added to the thrill.

Two weeks later, a satirical play received rave reviews in both performances. In the play, a doctor, who had been concerned about his patients eating too many turkey eggs and causing them to have heavy sexual fantasies, injected them with a truth serum. This caused each in turn to reveal they had always been oversexed.

The doctor in the play kept the syringe and the needle.

Two days later, one woman went into convulsions and became violent to the extent she had to be restrained and her husband complained of feeling spacey. She later died.

"Let's go for a ride," Carter said casually to Annie, in a tone more demanding than requesting. He led her to the Mercedes where Ken and Jess waited. In a moment he had left the compound and drove slowly to the east toward Sedona, with no particular goal in mind. Opening the conversation, he said to Annie, who sat behind Ken, "When Brenda left us, so to speak, she confessed to having a supply of poison of both liquid and powdered mushroom extracts. She told us where to find them. They were not there. Unfortunately, we can't interrogate her further, which leaves two suspects, Gregor and Bailey.

"The question to you, is this: The affected couple

had eaten breakfast. Were they also working in hy-dro afterwards?"

Annie said, "Only Judy. Mark was working the turkey farm."

Ken continued the questioning. "Annie, we need an honest answer. Has Jenny ever stolen produce from you?"

Annie blushed. "A lot of people . . . I mean . . ."

"It's a simple question. It has nothing to do with you and everything to do with her," Carter rejoined.

"Yes, she has," Annie admitted. "I spoke with her about it weeks ago and she promised she wouldn't do it again. I hate to call her a liar. She can't defend herself now, anyway."

"What were you picking," Jess asked from the back seated next to Annie.

"Tomatoes. Beth and I were planning to make pasta for dinner, with turkey dark meat optional," Annie answered.

"My theory is that maybe Judy stole a tomato or two and shared them with her husband," Carter con-jectured.

"What does that have to do with us sitting here in the car driving nowhere?" Annie accused, looking as though she might be ready to open the door and jump out.

"Was either Gregor or Bailey working that shift?" inquired Ken.

"After he got relieved of kitchen duty, Bailey doubled up working the greenhouses," Annie admit-ted.

Jess said, "You're thinking he somehow got to the tomatoes and poisoned one or more of them? What are the odds of Judy picking a poisoned tomato out of a pile?"

"Our bad guy might not care, or it might have happened some other way. What do I know? As long as somebody ate it, what does our poisoner care? What we need to do is to catch somebody doing it."

"I'm thinking airport security," Ken grinned a knowing smile, using a term obviously in reference to some experience shared between them.

"Right." Carter explained to Jess about how drug-sniffing dogs worked airports and border patrols around the world to ferret out drug smugglers, large and small.

Annie laughed, relieved to see the heat was off her and a chance loomed ahead to catch an evil person in their midst. The tomato thief and her husband had already paid their dues. "I love the idea. We'll need to keep him away from my food for a few days while you train Carla and the other dogs. Our criminal will probably be anxious to get back to his dirty work after a few days off. We can announce that the dogs will be walking into the greenhouses, supposedly at random times, looking for mice or whatever and make sure he's there one of the times when they are. We'll try it again if, we don't get him at first."

"If he's the one," Jess offered.

"No harm no foul," Ken said.

"Huh? Oh, another Topsider secret message," Jess said.

Annie inquired, "Can the dogs smell through a glass bottle?"

"I'm thinking more in terms of a plastic syringe," Carter replied, and made a U-turn heading back towards home.

Making her rounds on mice patrol three days later, Carla enjoyed the attention of every person in the greenhouse, even while she walked amongst them, up and down rows of plants, looking along edges and into corners, sniffing. When she came to the lawyer, she began to sniff around his pockets.

"Annie, what's Carla doing," Bailey cried.

Annie put took a step down from a stool she was using to check on a tier of spray-misted garlic. Wiping her hands she came over and laughed, hoping the dog would bite the man. "She's sniffing everything for mice. Don't ask me, ask the dog. Do you have a mouse in your pocket?"

"Nothing much." Bailey reached into his right-hand pocket and pulled out a syringe with a cap on the end of the needle point. "Oh, I forgot. It's still there from the play," he confessed sheepishly.

"That's a pretty big syringe," Annie remarked. "It's full, too."

Bailey scoffed. "It's just water. Besides, it had to be big so everyone in the audience could see it."

"Why do you still have a needle on it?" Annie asked, baiting him.

"To make it seem more realistic," he said, haltingly, caught in his own illogic. "It's capped so I don't stick myself. If it makes you happy, I'll remove it," he said, dropping his right hand to remove the needle with the left hand. Carla, apparently feeling threatened by the movement of the syringe toward her, bit him in the hand so hard the syringe splintered, crushing it into his palm and breaking a number of bones in his hand. He yelled loudly, drawing the attention of others, while blood ran freely from his wounds to stain the concrete floor of the structure.

Annie pulled out her radio and called for one of the doctors to bring a stitching kit and antiseptic, along with some forceps to pull pieces of plastic from a wound, sorry she hadn't wished for more. She also knew she had nothing solid on the man, circumstantial evidence at best. But the day was still young. First thing, tell Jess to get Bailey out of her greenhouses and keep him out. Put him on latrine duty, whatever. Jess put him back on kitchen duty.

With a bandaged right hand, Baily showed his determination by finishing a cleanup shift around the compound, a constant chore removing debris blown in from the surrounding forest, when he noticed Jess and Jay drive off in the ATV. The route they took suggested they were headed to the region of the Big House. He wanted to speak with her about more work she needed done to get on her good side, but it would have to wait. His legal mind understood a slight suspicion had been cast upon him. On the positive side, Annie was the one beating the drum, which could be taken with a grain of salt, considering her bias against him. *Isn't love wonderful?* he thought.

Within the hour the couple returned and moments later Jess went to speak with Carter and Bailey saw the drone take off. Something was up. Then the storm hit and shut things down. He was about to approach her the next day when he saw her go into the meeting hall with the council members.

At last, no longer able to contain himself, he ensured a coincidental meeting with her on the street, mentioning that he had seen her leave with Jay the day before and wanted to know if everything was all right.

Although Bailey had his faults, one could always trust him to keep a secret. Carefully choosing her words, Jess mentioned the cocaine, thinking it interesting, but no big deal. She left out the part about the cooking materials. Only a few remained privy to the secret.

When she told him about the drugs, Bailey had to look down momentarily to contain his feelings. When he looked up, all he said was, "Oh, how much did you find?"

"We think 20 bags."

Bailey's mouth turned down in surprise. He said, casually, as though if he were brushing a piece of lint from his clothing. "That's a lot. What are you going to do with it all?"

"We don't know yet. Maybe give some of it to the doctors." she answered.

"That's a good idea. Well, the storm left quite

a mess. Think I'll go back to cleaning up," Bailey concluded.

Give it a few days and it might be time to seek medical attention about some various aches and pains that seem to be cropping up. Could the good doctor prescribe anything for the pain? It kept him awake all night. He wouldn't even mind taking something experimental, if the doctor thought it would help.

12

Danny wanted his own office away with a separate door away from visitor. The office didn't have to be much, a reclining armchair and a small desk would do. He'd be happy to read by lantern light or by a dim bulb.

He'd thought about it for a long time ever since the discovery of the treasure in the loft. Pulling out his medical books, he began to read about the medicinal uses of natural pain killers. He learned that, at one time, the opium poppy was happily cultivated in Southeastern China, Myanmar, Laos, Thailand, Afghanistan, Pakistan, and other more isolated regions. A volcanic eruption occurred in the island chain or Sumatra and the name of the volcano was Tambora. The cloud from the single eruption affected global climate to such an extent it caused a cholera outbreak in India, enough snowfall in England to lead Mary Shelley to insert snow-related scenes in her novel *Frankenstein,* and opium poppies to be cultivated in southeastern China because of the poppy's climate-tolerance.

Opioids such as heroin, morphine and codeine are derived from the opium poppy. Fine. His interest didn't lie in history, only in medicinal uses. What he did find relevant was that well over a century ago, laudanum, a mixture of alcohol and opium, was so effective and popular as a painkiller and numbing agent it became addictive. Not only did the public at large become addicted to it, but so did the pharmacists who concocted the mixture, and even the doctors who prescribed it. For obvious reasons, a number of members of congress refused to vote for the ban of laudanum to become the first drug to be regulated in the United States. Furthermore, one of his professors had told the class that the first Coca Colas made back in the late 19th Century were in small 6-oz bottles, each of which contained 3.5 grams of cocaine.

Turning his attention to another class of drugs, he researched cocaine, one he remembered well from his medical school training. Touted as an excellent topical anesthetic, cocaine was found to be a highly effective vasoconstrictive agent and related to lidocaine, which he and Alex had used for years in UL-One as a numbing agent for dental procedures and as a topical pain killer. Lidocaine, a natural derivative of cocaine, served as a nerve-blocking agent. Lidocaine had a natural origin and was not synthesized *de novo* in the laboratory. Therefore, it could be obtained during their semi-annual requests for supplies from topside in the old days. Cocaine, however, could not be supplied by Ken's business for the simple reason that the purity could not be trusted, nor could a supply be guaranteed. Contaminants frequently proved to be injurious when used in a clinical setting.

Some three decades separated Danny from medical school and his use of cocaine to stay awake all night to study. A few years of professional practice followed by 20 years of underground hibernation cured him of this practice.

Now he possessed a kilo of cocaine and it hadn't yet been cut, at least as far as he could tell with his best magnifying glass. There were no corn starch particles, no baking soda crystals, only a crystalline coke crushed into a powder. If it were diluted 10-fold there would be over 22,000 grams and for whatever the going price had been per gram, it multiplied out to a lot of money back then. And that was only one of 20 bags. What to do? He touched his finger to the white powder and rubbed it against his gums to feel an instant numbing effect and a slight feeling of well-being seconds later, which dissipated shortly. No wonder natives of Colombia and Peru and many other countries habitually chewed cocoa leaves .

Leaning back in his chair, Danny tried to digest the enormity of it all. He decided to read more. *If you can't make a decision, make no decision at all until you have more information.* With civilization destroyed and without access to lidocaine anymore, he desperately needed a substitute and, hands down, cocaine fit the description as the perfect replacement.

He also had the concern about his inability to do anything about the poisonings, feeling hamstrung. He could do nothing to prevent them, and little more than nothing to cure them. He could only report what had happened, something the poisoned person already knew. Therefore, it might be best if somebody else worried about it. He had other problems to solve.

By the time Danny finished reading, he had decided to use cocaine as a topical anesthetic for numbing of gums during dentistry, inhalation therapy to reduce inflammation of the respiratory tract, and as an injectable for chronic and more severe injuries. It wouldn't hurt to ingest it either for a temporary boost of self-confidence, increased vigilance, and well-being to certain patients who complained of anxiety. Self-medication was a given. Because the drug dissolved easily in mucous membranes and water, Danny came to a conclusion: It might be a good idea to drink a lot more water.

13

Those few knowledgeable about the existence of the drugs decided against informing the populace of the discovery, unsure what direction the public might take the knowledge, especially if it were known how much natural medication could be at their disposal. No worries. The good doctor would look out for them.

If anybody knew his people, Danny did. He could easily count those who suffered different degrees of trauma after coming to the surface, who had arguments at home with their spouses, who had shifted psychological stress into physical stresses, or vice versa, or who lost sleep, or even turned to violence like Brenda had. To his way of thinking, playing in the band or playing chess, checkers, or board games did not address the underlying stress wrought by surface life to the populace at large, himself included.

He had been handed the means to treat the problems at his discretion and that's what he began to do. After he took a snort, just to ensure the purity of the product, the rush hit him immediately. He stayed high for longer than he expected. What also surprised him was the clean come-down. He had no lingering stupor, only a rapid return to reality. He could fairly conclude that he had in his possession the best of the best.

Danny obtained a couple of small glass containers from the city stores and filled them with the powder, adding water. He began to use it topically on burns incurred by the kitchen staff, on scrapes and bruises incurred by construction personnel, and on patients who required dental work. His new method of inhalation therapy using a 'new vaso-constricting agent' worked wonders on persons complaining of respiratory distress. His popularity increased and the medical facility found itself busy. In order to reduce the patient load, he assigned his two nurses in training to make the rounds each evening to keep up with demand.

To the public, it seemed as though a respiratory virus had appeared. The un-afflicted included most members of the governing council, who held a private session in the meeting hall. Alex and A.J. also attended. The youth, now in his late teens, had shown a propensity for medicine from the early years and clearly expressed concern about the present epidemic.

Through the double-paned windows, blowing dust could be seen to cause passers-by to cover their heads. Blowing dust could not be good for their lungs. Jess said, "What's a rundown of our present epidemic, Alex?"

The doctor replied, "It's the same thing everybody knows, we started a few weeks ago with only a few patients and it spread atypically."

"With another difference my father is leaving out," A.J. contributed.

"Which is?" Carter inquired, already knowing the answer, but he wanted to hear it from the medical staff.

"There are no symptoms, only complaints of symptoms," A.J. continued. "No runny noses, sneezing, headaches, phlegm or mucous drainage, maybe a slight cough on occasion, no lung involvement, as far as we can tell by stethoscope."

"Who was the first case?" Beth asked.

Alex responded, "It's hard to say because we've always have some respiratory complaints, even underground. Understandably, we've had more complaints since we moved to the surface. About the best we can do is to go by the level of frequency and even that's difficult to ascertain, because there appeared to be a slow rise, followed by an increasing rise, rather than an exponential increase one would expect when a virus is at work."

Alex added, defensively, "Just because we lived underground didn't mean we didn't get colds and couldn't track the epidemiology. Some of you went to Flag a couple of times recently. Do you think you might have brought something back with you? Oh, and poisonings are continuing, which, to us, is the more important focus. The medical staff is wondering if there is an issue here."

Ken shook his head vigorously back and forth. "Forget the last part. If we had brought it back, we should be the first ones affected and none of us are."

The room remained silent after the exchange. "Where do we go from here?" Carter asked of anyone who might have any opinion at all.

"Not much we can do to permanently fix the virus problem. We'll have to let it play out and see where it leads," Alex shrugged.

"By the way, how's your father?" asked Jess. "We're all concerned."

"Dad's got a sinus congestion and wants to stay isolated in his office as much as possible. He doesn't want anybody to catch what he has. He even has his meals brought to him," Alex remarked.

A.J. interjected, "He does recommend we provide deep steam therapy to the patients for their temporary relief."

Glancing at the blowing dust outside, Jess admitted, "I'll have to confess I do get more congested up here than I ever did back home. I might have to give this steam therapy a try, even if it's for temporary relief. Tell your dad to keep up the good work."

Alex passed on the message before he became poisoned and lay close to death.

14

There is never a good time for a disease to run rampant, but some times are worse than others. This is especially true when a population is already suffering from a purported respiratory contagion. Jess never considered that the method of treatment may have led to the contagion. This time complaints were backed up by clinical symptoms, which disabled virtually the entire workforce. With Alex barely hanging on to life, to Jess it was clear that not only had he been poisoned, but he had also caught this viral strain going around.

Still, Jess was mystified. She'd read everything she could about the workings of DNA, RNA, and the properties of The Mars Virus. She spent hours reading the medical books the doctors had on store, many of which she had contributed. She came to the conclusion that everything with a genetic code can have variants. Siders were variants of native DNA in animal life and although viruses were not alive because they could not self-reproduce, those with either DNA or RNA might have their own variants, which might permit them to be infectious. Even *E. coli* had its toxic variants.

At the time Randolph and his team were heavily engaged in their research, they concluded that all viruses had become inactivated simply because The Mars Virus bound to their DNA making in unable to infect other cells. Given the presence of a variant, it was almost as though something had caused a weakening of the immune response. This is with the exception of certain members of the medical staff, along with the members of the executive council. Danny appeared to be most seriously afflicted and insisted he be left alone where he could remain until he recovered. Danny was the hardest hit of anyone, now too weak to prepare his daily batch of medicinal steam, which he made from natural herbs. Initially, he did find it to be of relief, but soon, the *only* thing it provided for him was a desire to ingratiate himself with more.

After a week of illness, the new virus appeared to weaken its hold on the body as the immune system regained its full function. By the tenth day, recovery was complete with the exception of the only true medical doctor.

Carter had always told Jess that if there weren't solid reasons for the contrary, it's best to go with your gut feeling and to her, things didn't add up. An inconsequential detail to one person may lead to a major breakthrough in a case. Tired of getting information third hand, she decided to visit the good doctor in person for a conversation, hoping he might shed some light on the virus issue recently plaguing the population. Still some distance away, she saw Bailey leaving the medical center and thought little of it. People came and went for various reasons.

When Jess entered the medical center, she found Danny alone. She had never seen anyone look worse, not even the man she had shot while two dogs ripped meat from his legs. His eyes were sunken and watery, his skin pasty. He spoke as though he had a clamp on his nose. In addition, his terrible deep cough was evidence the new virus had deeply infected him.

Once perfunctory greetings were exchanged, Jess asked if Bailey was all right because she had seen him leave. Danny told her he was under treatment, but wouldn't reveal anything further. When she inquired about his general treatments for the community at large, Danny went over the same party line everybody else knew, with no revelations. She needed to get more specific and start from the beginning. "Your patients came here and you provide them with steam inhalation therapy. Right?"

Danny nodded, nonchalantly.

"And it has natural herbs? Right?"

Danny had nothing to hide regarding his medical practice. "Only one," he said.

"Which is?"

Danny shrugged, and pulled open a drawer to reveal one of the bags of cocaine with a portion of it missing. Jess knew the bag. Along with Jay, she had discovered it. Both Jay and Carter had schooled her about its historical usage around the world. Holding up a finger for Danny to wait a minute, she pulled out her reading slate and spent several minutes researching the effect of cocaine on the immune system, including an increased susceptibility to bacterial and viral infections.

Jess was shocked. Not only had the doctor used the substance on a large percentage of their population, he had become addicted.

Without shaming him for his negligence, and with Alex too ill to be of assistance, she opted to discuss it with Carter later so they could all make an informed decision about how to deal with the problem. Something else didn't ring right. "Danny, where is the rest of your staff?"

"Working their shifts," he answered, nasally.

"Of course, silly question." Jess felt the fool. She had revealed part of their discovery to someone who didn't need to know and it had come back to bite her. In the strictest sense, he never did reveal her secret to another, only used the knowledge to his advantage. Live and learn.

Danny Gomez, the only surface-trained medical doctor in the city, died later that night. Even at the end of civilization, drugs and viruses played a hand, serving as two scourges of mankind. No autopsy would be necessary.

PART TWO

1

"He couldn't find you so he gave it to me to give to you," Beth said at the house after dinner. She handed Jess a two page document. Jess looked at it, pursed her lips and gave it to Jay, who quickly scanned the pages, raised his eyebrows, and gave them back to Beth.

Jess said, "We may have bigger problems than this. We'll talk about it at home tonight."

With the day winding down, Jess figured this was as good a time any. "Carla, go get Annie," she commanded, opening the door. The dog ran next door and scratched on the trailer's door. Two minutes later they both returned. Annie had thrown a sweater over her bathrobe. "What's up?" she asked.

"A lawsuit in the name of Charles Bailey," Jess stated.

She had everybody's attention. Carter stopped playing with the children and the dog, Jay and Wei stopped babbling with their electronics, Ken and

Beth put down their books.

Not too pleased at what she was about to convey, Jess shook the pages in her hand as if shooing away a fly. "He's claiming defamation because there is clear evidence we damaged his character. He wants this house as retribution. According to Bailey, he can own the city and everything in it, if a jury finds in his favor. It states that he was an outstanding citizen who got viciously attacked by Carla. Subsequent to the attack, he has limited function of his right hand. The injuries he received as a result of this wanton act of violence by an unleashed dog limits his ability to perform hard physical labor, although his cleaning activities at the Big House should continue indefinitely because they involve light activities, which, by the way, were recommend by us."

"Whatever. We caught him dead-to-rights," Annie declared.

"No, you caught him with a syringe and a needle that he still had in his pocket because he used it in the play," Jess corrected.

"He was going to inject it into some fruit," Annie insisted.

"So you say," Jess countered.

"He began to hallucinate from the broken syringe in his hand shortly afterward. Everybody saw that and it lasted for over two days," Wei inserted.

"Sheer coincidence. He claims he got poisoned like everyone else from the last meal he ate," Jess said.

"The syringe had poison in it. I saw it," Annie

cried.

"So you say," Jess repeated.

"Not only that, but three days after the incident with the syringe, he volunteered to go back on kitchen duty and you let him. Then Alex got poisoned," Annie pounded, relentlessly.

"Same answer."

"We know he took the stash from the cave after he reported Brenda's presence there," Beth declared.

"Circumstantial evidence," Jess countered, playing devil's advocate. He brought us the stash, remember? We even rewarded him for turning her in, showing our confidence in him. In fact, the two jars he turned in to us that he took from the cave had no poison in them, as far I could tell by taste. I could only test for psilocybin—that's a simple chemical test, and it was absent. In itself, even a negative result means nothing because the Mars Virus is famous for screwing up chemical reactions. We don't have the means to check for anything else, although I did feed some of what he brought to the crickets and they had no adverse effects. Chuck also said he was sorry about having to do this, but the law is the law."

Jay contributed, "We need hard evidence or a good prosecuting attorney. If we searched his room at the Big House, he could call it a witch hunt and if we found anything while doing so, he could claim we planted it."

"The guy is a nut case," Ken said.

"He's also high on coke," said Jay.

"Doctor's prescription. Danny told me. He wouldn't tell me what it was for."

Rarely emotional, Wei stated flatly, "Back off. Suppose we file charges of our own against him, like serious criminal charges."

After a moment's reflection, Carter said, "I like it. Because there is only one attorney in town, we put Chuck in the crosshairs. When word gets out about that, he won't be too smug. Hopefully, the citizens will start to consider two sides to the coin."

Ken said, "Since Annie caught him, the poisonings didn't stop. What now?"

"If it's him, he won't use the syringe trick anymore," Jess said. "We found nothing in the cave when we cleaned it out, other than a bunch of jars and a little cooking paraphernalia. I'm telling you, other than me, I'm willing to bet Benda's the only person who knows how to make the stuff and do it right. We found no poison anywhere. I don't care what she told us. It's hard to convict somebody when you lack evidence."

Carter suggested, "Jay, Wei, can you begin drawing up criminal charges against him? Use the suit against us as a model. We don't have anything solid on him for a counter-suit."

Wei smiled, cutely. "You don't need anything solid. Based on everything we considered and everything Jess negated, we'll use those as claims against him. Let him prove us wrong."

"You thinking what I'm thinking?" Ken asked.

"Yep," Carter replied.

"I probably thought it first, though," Ken returned.

"No doubt."

"What are you guys talking about?" Jess said, out of patience for word games.

Carter explained, "Bailey sure came out of nowhere fast. Suddenly, he's going for the whole enchilada. Where's the last place you'd look for the stash? Granted, he's not a chemist. We pulled all the hotplates and cooking utensils from the loft and the cave, so someone would have to start from scratch. Rule out Brenda telling someone else about her pet project for a lot of reasons. I'll bet he kept the poison and gave us nothing solid. We'll never get away with conspiracy against Bailey, because he'd call it a setup or sour grapes."

Wei said, "Remember, if Bailey is involved, he isn't a trained terrorist. Although he may get off on reading about them, I see him as a dangerous wannabe who has delusions of grandeur, which, by the way, are being stoked by drugs if Jess's suspicions are correct."

One week later, high on painkiller, Bailey received his own lawsuit. He contacted the city council as an attorney representing the defendant who happens to be himself, the mayor and why wasn't he informed of this clandestine meeting. He requested an arbitration hearing with all parties present.

Jess would chair the meeting at the request of the other council members. To her, the quandary was that Brenda had not described the containers she had left behind and either Gregor or Bailey could have taken them. In theory, so could she or Carter, or Ken for that matter, because they all knew the perp had moved the operation to the cave. If Gregor had a dark side, he kept it buried so deep no one had ever captured a glimpse of it.

Before the meeting came to order, Jess announced that Ken would be late. He was out with the two dogs looking for mice.

Everyone filed into the meeting room at the same time. Bailey faced the council members gathered in a row behind two tables slid together. Gregor sat alone in a separate chair to their right, serving as Sergeant at Arms. Overall, Bailey had some things to sort out, but still felt comfortable while he assessed the situation. He had known four of the members for many years, while the others were Topsiders. If it came down to a vote, it would surely swing in his favor. This was no different than facing a jury. It all came down to persuading them to see his side. Been there, done that.

He wouldn't have minded if Brenda had been there. They had gotten along famously. Unfortunately, she had mysteriously disappeared. It didn't take a genius to relate her disappearance to coincide with his reporting that she was the one behind the poisonings. What made him more than a little nervous was the thought that, while he was accused of high crimes, the other side had done something bad to Brenda. Had they turned her loose, tortured her to death, or shot her? If so, he faced a formidable foe.

In summary, it sounded like the Topsiders, Ken and Carter, had made the arrangements for her disappearance. They could be flies in his ointment. On the other hand, he had the law on his side. His experience told him the opposition often came across aggressively at first for purposes of negotiation, then backed off. No worries.

Bailey had a look of fear mixed with righteous indignation in his eyes. *The consummate actor*, Jess thought. She wondered what was going through his mind. She also wondered whether her small-town mentality had taken over her thought process in that a person is considered guilty depending on what most people believed. As a powerful force, belief can override common sense and it had nothing to do with intelligence.

Bailey held a single sheet of paper in front of him and cleared his throat, doing his best to look officious and in charge. He said, "This isn't strictly legal phraseology, however you are the governing body, the police, and the jailers, so I guess it really doesn't matter how it's worded, so I'll let that slide."

Reading from the paper, he said, "This matter concerns a complaint by the citizens of Sekah City against Charles Bailey. Mr. Bailey is accused of the following crimes: terrorism against the state, murder, attempted murder, sedition, preparation and distribution of weapons of mass destruction, concealment of such weapons, conspiracy, and theft. Further charges will be brought against Mr. Bailey in additional documents to be submitted following subsequent hearings on the matter.

"Mr. Bailey is entitled to legal representation who may offer his defense in a jury trial. This document is signed by all members of the city council. Did I read that as you presented it to me?"

Jess gave the briefest of nods and replied, "Yes, you did. As a slight amendment to your statement, we are the jury. There is no tomorrow. What would you like to say on behalf of your client?"

The defendant looked as though he had been sucker punched. Reading the charges against him had caused a chill to run through him, hearing then in a court of law added another dimension to his fear.

Gathering himself, Bailey, pulled out another sheet of paper from a small briefcase and said, "Our defense is the same as the lawsuit brought against the city in that there is no evidence to prove Mr. Bailey committed any wrongdoing. Our belief is that a jury will concur. Clearly nefarious activities are afoot. This entire matter smacks of both a witch hunt and supposition. There is no evidence of poison or mushrooms that can be associated with him. Therefore, I propose that, as responsible parties representing this city, you drop all charges against the defendant, and in a show of good faith, he will drop the lawsuit against you. That is, under one condition."

He had them over a barrel.

"So you're disavowing this proposed trade-off?" Carter asked the defendant.

"Absolutely. Let a jury decide," Bailey insisted, looking directly at the others from Beth at one end to

Jay at the other. He knew they had nothing on him. Nobody could prove a single thing and they knew it. He only needed to stick with the party line. It didn't take a genius to see they were shaking the tree to see what fell out—game playing to muddy the waters.

2

The door opened and Ken walked in, along with A.J. Ken said, "We can settle this matter now. Gregor, if you please."

Still seated, Gregor reached down into a small case he carried and carefully lifted out a jar of liquid and another of chopped mushroom segments. Ken said, "Are these the ones you brought back from the cave right after you reported Brenda had been there?"

"Looks like them," Bailey answered, peering at the jars from several feet away. *What was up with that?*

"Interesting. What do you think these are?" Ken queried, pulling two more similar jars from his own satchel. Both were empty. He walked in front of the council members to display one in each hand, then brought them over to the attorney who blanched.

Bailey declared, "What are these? Where did you get them?"

Ken asked, pointing at A.J. "Do you trust these this man?"

"Well, yeah, uh, I guess," Bailey stammered, uncertain of the path Ken was leading him down. He felt as though he were the accused on the witness stand with nowhere to hide, not the lawyer representing his client, albeit one and the same.

"That's good to know because he was with me when we found these containers in your dresser buried underneath your shirts," Ken smiled. "We also found this large baggie of cocaine. Looks like you came prepared to steal from Danny and that's what you did."

"Well, that's inadmissible, I mean, he gave me that for pain."

Ken replied, "You don't know what pain is. It's called probable cause and we're now adding conspiracy to defraud to the list of charges against you. Madam Secretary, are you recording this?"

Without setting down her pencil, Beth replied, "Every word."

"Wait a minute," Bailey said. "Can I see those?" He stood to walk over to Ken, at which point Gregor also stood, watching closely. He was armed, as was Ken, who nodded to Gregor as if to say, "I got this," and handed the containers to Bailey.

"Do you recognize these? Ken asked.

They had him. Time to fall on his sword. No, not yet. Bailey scoffed, "Somebody put them there."

Carter shot, "Where's the stuff that was in them?"

Bailey reiterated, "I'll tell you again. I never saw

them before."

Carter said, "Here's what we think, Chuck. You took the ones that had poison and a set that did not have poison and gave us the clean ones. The ones you gave the council were two screw-cap jars, the ones Gregor is showing. Each of the four contained about six ounces of either liquid or solid."

"What reason would I have to keep a couple of empty jars?" Bailey complained.

He had a point, asking the question so rhetorically that nobody thought a legitimate answer could be forthcoming.

Angry beyond measure, Jess had difficulty maintaining her composure. They had all been used and abused by a con artist, a demented man working to bring down their society for his amusement. There could be no rehabilitation.

When she told Carter about how she had shared the information with the attorney and how badly she felt about it, he told her, "You're supposed to make mistakes and learn from them. It's part of the survival mechanism. You're supposed to be stung by a bad decision. The memory is your safeguard against doing it again. Don't go beyond that to punish yourself. You must remain your own best friend."

The memory of that sting brought her to say the words that would have been painful to the girl of old. In the light of a new day, she looked forward to saying them, even if they did apply to a person she'd seen all her life. If she had learned anything, it was the harsh reality of survival in a real world, not a baby sheltered from germs. She said, "Frankly, I think you're lying. You might want to find a good defense attorney. Good luck with that.

"Let it be known that the death penalty is one option the jury will decide upon. The other is ejection. Our meager community is not set up for anything in-between. Although, now that I think of it, having you clean toilets for the rest of your life, as your sole duty, is not off the table. For that, there is no going back. There is a piece missing in you.

"Mr. Bailey, you *are* going to tell us what you did with the contents of those jars."

Bailey seemed to deflate, not in defeat, but in victory. He sat back in his chair and calmly informed the board of his legal rights and that he refused to testify against himself, adding, "However, I think we can come to an agreement where everyone is satisfied."

Bailey believed he had them up against the wall. Who knew the law better than he? In a minute, the law would win out. He would be free and own a nice house, as decreed by the city council. His confidence soared.

Carter decided to change direction and asked, "Charles, where did you go to law school?"

"Huh, what . . . ?"

"It's a simple question," Carter said.

"Arizona State University School of Law," he replied. He felt safe with that answer. He'd lost count of how many times graduates from that school had defended him over the years and kept him out of jail or had successfully filed suits in his name. He'd learned from his parents the lucrative game of moving from one high-end home to another, soon finding fault with the home and suing the homeowner and his insurance company for injuries and damages. After an out-of-court settlement, he'd move on to a different city or a different state. Certainly, after a background like that, he'd learned the ins and outs of the legal system, both ends of it. When the world went south, he needed to reinvent himself. He moved to the only place possible, the underground city. What could be more advantageous than proclaiming himself to be a lawyer? Let them prove otherwise.

Annie requested, "Charles, we're even wondering whether you went to college at all. We all remember our best and worst teachers, our best and worst subjects. Could you please share with us your experiences in several of your university classes, law school or otherwise? We'd like to hear more about your earlier life before you joined UL-One. Take your time." She looked at the others, who also nodded encouragingly for Bailey to relate that portion of his life.

"Why? What kind of question is that?" Bailey replied, defensively. This wasn't going well.

"It's not a question," Annie replied, not so sweetly this time, at the end of her rope. "It's a request."

Tired of playing word games, she amped it up a notch. "Here's our take Charles. We were wondering whether you actually went to law school or you made up the whole story. Prove us wrong."

"I don't have to do that," Bailey said, standing his ground. "It's irrelevant."

Remembering what Jess had told him and Carter about Danny supplying Bailey with cocaine, Ken said, "Enough. He's got a slimy self-satisfying smirk I don't like. Could be the drugs he's been taking. Or maybe he's living out a television drama and maybe he doesn't understand the rules."

"Hey, any medications I took were definitely doctor authorized," Bailey began to whine, somewhat nasally.

Carter stood, as did Ken. "Gregor, do you want to watch?"

Gregor stood. "I'm always willing to learn," he replied.

"This is called retribution, Charles," Carter said, succinctly.

"I'm going with you. Meeting adjourned," Jess declared.

Carter said, "I don't think . . . "

"We'll talk outside," Jess said.

Without a word from the council members, all of whom were thoroughly disgusted by the actions of the accused, watched as Gregor and Ken took Bailey, who had a look of bafflement, each grabbing one of his arms.

"What are you doing? Where are we going," Bailey cried, angrily, self-righteously. Apparently, these testosterone-laden jerks needed to be educated. Time to play hardball. Putting on his intimidation hat, Bailey declared, "This is still the United States of America. I have my constitutional rights and as an attorney specializing in criminal cases, I'm informing you that you face severe consequences, should you pursue this matter further in regards to . . . "

"What's he talking about?" Gregor asked, scratching his head.

"I have no idea," Carter admitted. "There is no United States and there is no constitution. There is also no Fifth Amendment, so don't go there."

Once outside, Carter didn't give his wife a chance to say a word. Instead, he offered, "Don't say it. You have every right to watch this. They were your people he killed. Okay? Let's go."

Jess saved her rage and walked alongside him to his truck to find Ken and Gregor in the back seat with Bailey looking diminutive seated between the two big men.

Carter started the truck and drove out of the compound, turning south down a narrow dirt road. Nobody spoke for a period of time. Beads of sweat broke out on Bailey's forehead.

Turning to Bailey, Ken explained, "We're going someplace quiet where we can have a one-way negotiation until the four of us are satisfied. Unfortunately, you will not be quite as pleased when we're finished."

Looking over Bailey to the man seated at his right, Ken said, "Gregor, "You're not going to throw up again are you?"

"Come on, Ken, those were mutilated bodies," returned Gregor, playing along. Besides, he only said he felt like throwing up at the sight of all the bodies at the restaurant. He didn't actually do it.

"Why should I tell you anything if all you're going to do is kill me?" Bailey queried, showing remarkable restraint in keeping the quaver out of his voice, hoping beyond hope these men had a trace of humanity left in them. What that exactly meant, he wasn't quite certain, but hopefully, it would relate to his survival.

"Who said anything about killing you? In fact, we're going to do everything in our power to ensure you stay alive," Ken answered.

Jess turned to the left to stare at Bailey. At the same time she reached behind her to remove her gun from its waistband holster. She laid it on the armrest.

Carter grinned. *She's learning.*

Standing side-by-side, Jess and Bailey would be the same height. That's where the similarity ended. The attorney's hands and body were soft, accustomed to a life of soft living. Jess's muscles were hardened, her hands calloused from years of outdoor construction work. "The first question is: Where's the rest of what was in those jars?" she demanded.

Bailey's look of fear at seeing the gun morphed into a smile. "You see, you want something and I want something. So let's make a deal."

"He's reading books that are a bad influence on him that have nothing to do with our present reality," Carter said. "Gregor, please explain to our guest about reality."

Gregor grabbed both sides of Bailey's right knee

with his large left hand, his fingers squeezing as hard as he could. He did not let go despite the attorney's attempts to claws his hand away while screaming in pain until Jess nodded for Gregor to release his iron grip long seconds later.

"His voice is like my wife's when she sees a mouse?" Gregor stated, objectively, without mirth.

"Maybe you can write a love song about it," Carter offered, almost as though he were a gangster reading a script in a bad movie after shooting down his opponents.

Recovering momentarily, through tears of pain, Bailey announced, "A confession under coercion is not legal . . . "

"You just won't let it go, will you, Charles? We're not coercing you, we're encouraging you," Carter said. He looked to Jess who nodded to Gregor who began to squeeze again until Bailey began to inform the others once again about his rights and for them to wait until he reported their actions to authorities.

Jess nodded to Gregor to stop and said, "Ken, your turn."

Seated to Bailey's left, Ken grabbed the left knee with his right and bore down. Only inches separated their faces. Ken did not let go and Jess did not nod for him to do so. Instead, she pulled a fingernail file from somewhere and carefully checked to ensure her nails were kept short enough and no dirt had gotten beneath them.

Gregor, who typically remained silent and did his job, had his own words to say. "You poisoned a doctor? We can't hurt you enough for that."

"Is he all right?" Bailey gasped through tears.

"Thank you for asking, Charles, that was very thoughtful of you. He's recovering,"

Ken said, squeezing harder.

"All right, all right," Bailey screamed, as Gregor grabbed his left knee again, his face covered with sweat, his shirt soaked. Bailey confessed through tears and gasping sobs that he was never a lawyer, and that he had added the mixtures to the turkey feed.

Gregor looked over at Jess who had racked a round in the gun, to point it between Bailey's eyes. She had a look of such disdain, such contempt, that her face flushed. After this, she swore to herself she would scrub herself thoroughly to remove the filth of his presence.

Carter radioed Jay and informed him of the information. "Take the dogs to sniff it out and have them check every other food supply. We'll wait here until you report back," he said, stopping the car in the middle of the road.

Ken rolled down the side window and looked out. "Looks like another storm coming in. Don't they ever end?" he observed.

Carter leaned for forward to look up and around. "Yep, nasty one, big hailstones this time. Those could hurt you, if you don't find shelter." Looking in the rearview mirror at Bailey, he said, "I don't mean to interrupt your love affair back there, but you were saying something about your rights." Bailey swung his head back and forth as a clear indication he had nothing further to say on the subject.

Carter reached into the console and selected a Willie Nelson CD, which he inserted into the player. "We might as well have some fun while we wait for Jay to call back. You remember Willie, don't you, Chuck?"

Bailed nodded vigorously. Anything to agree.

"Wait, Carter," Jess said, "First play my favorite song, the one you sent me way back when. You know, *The Battle Hymn of the Republic* by the Mormon Tabernacle Choir, where they sing about the Lord's terrible swift sword."

Forty minutes later, with Gregor's left hand casually resting on Bailey's knee, Jay called, as the first large drops of rain splatted on the windshield. He explained, "It wasn't in their present feed. He added it to the stock. It's ruined. What we have will buy us another week, then we'll be in a bind. That was all we could find."

Carter signed off. Turning to Bailey, he said, "You're a pretender, a person who couldn't hold down a job, a person who wanted to start a new life totally based on lies so you could get attention, like putting lipstick on a pig. You got to believe your own fantasies. You're FUBAR, Chuck. You're fucked up beyond repair. Your parents brought you up wrong."

Without waiting for an answer, Jess pounded in the nail harder. Maybe this was overkill. She didn't care. She had definitely developed a cruel, no, sadistic, streak. It takes one to know one. The baton had passed from Brenda to Bailey. The relay had to come to an end. She'd sort it out later. "You're the worst kind of loser. As of this moment, you've been convicted of murder, attempted murder, child endangerment, cruelty to animals, and terrorism charges. How's that working out for you, Charles?"

Bailey's face turned red. He had never been so excoriated. This bunch of sadists had hit him in his heart and soul. Suddenly, he had the urge to pee. Jess did not try to hide the malice in her voice when she spit, "Do you have any idea how much filth like you disgusts me?"

Ken had never seen Jess like this, nobody had. Angry, yes, on the verge of being out of control, no. Usually things came to blows long before words like this were spoken. Sensing that either she or Carter was preparing to literally rip the man's face off, Ken intervened. He wasn't completely satisfied with Bailey's explanations. He needed more information before anything else happened. "Next question. Why did you switch the jars? Why did you kill people and cause so much pain and suffering? It had to be exciting."

Rubbing both knees, Bailey's lower lip trembled in fear. Carter and the others had stripped him to the bone. "At first I thought it was terrible what Brenda had done. At the same time, her ideas sounded ingenious. I admired her in a way and thought I might have a little fun."

"You kept doing it knowing you could cause death?" Carter asked. *This is over the top.*

"I guess I used too much," Bailey said simplistically, as though he were talking to a class of third graders who couldn't understand English. "After Annie caught me with the syringe, I couldn't think of any new way to use it except to maybe give it to the dogs or the turkeys. After I got sewn up, I was so mad that I went to the second greenhouse and rubbed some stuff onto pieces of fruit with a rag. That's when a couple of people died. I guess I used too much. I thought I could get something out of it if I played my cards right. When I went back on the food line, I put it in Alex's food, but honestly, I didn't know it was him until it was too late."

Bailey came up for air, adding, "I mean, a man can make a mistake, can't he? That's the truth. I'm really sorry. Can we go back now?"

You can't make it up. This human has morphed into a delusional killer who only pretends to have remorse. "Absolutely," Carter said, almost in a whisper, the opposite of screaming. He turned the car around, adding, "Gregor, help our guest out so he can understand our legal system."

Gregor got out and walked around to the passenger side. He opened the door and grabbing Bailey by the arm and the scruff of his neck, dragged a thoroughly confused man out onto the roadway. Bailey tried to stand and collapsed in pain. His knees didn't work. A look of understanding came over him when Gregor got back in and closed the door. Carter rolled down his window and said, "The camp is five miles back up the road. As soon as we get back I'm going to send the dogs down here to look for you."

Carter was about to drive off when he paused to answer a call on his radio. He listened a moment and said "Will do."

"I got this," Jess said. She leaned across the console and across her husband to tell the seated man, "Annie says for you to have a nice day."

Carter drove away, feeling for Gregor, knowing that Annie would insist her son give her every second of the details in both English and Russian. That way she could hear the story twice.

Bailey felt confident they would return for him. He reached into his pocket to pull out the small vial that he had prepared some time ago for an emergency. This definitely qualified as one. The problem lay in the fact that he had been high when he prepared it and couldn't remember if he had put coke in it or magic mushroom powder for one last poisoning, or both. In the dim light of the oncoming storm, he couldn't tell whether it was white, off-white, or a mixture of the two. *What the hell. I have faith in my judgment.* He unscrewed the top, held the vial upside down into his nose, and inhaled deeply.

On the return trip, Gregor offered, "Maybe we should let him stew in his own juice."

"Fuck that," Jess spat. "I like Carter's idea. In addition to Carla and Riki, we've got six other intelligent dogs in the community who can follow orders. One of them belongs to Annie. I'll ask her if she wants her pet to lead a pack down here for a training session. That said, we're going to give Bailey an hour or so to reflect upon his life, then I'm sending him a number of going away presents, courtesy of the survivors.

3

Lying in bed, sleepless, Jess didn't like the anxiety that had overcome her for the past several hours. At first she ascribed it to the nonstop recordings she replayed in her mind of conversations with Bailey—things she had said and done, maybe should have said and done. These were intermingled with her last memories of Brenda, of how they had ordered her to stand up and start walking down the riverbank away from the city and to watch out for wild animals that could appear at any time. As a couple, they watched her follow the directive until she had appeared as a speck in the distance.

Shoving those seemingly endless thoughts aside, she tried to trace her anxiety to its source and realized it wasn't her alone that radiated nervous energy. In fact, the dogs seemed skittish. The more she thought about it, the more things came into focus.

The daytime temperature reached the low 70s, an insane amount of warmth for the area, according to what Carter had told her, akin to virtually constant temperatures underground. Even the cricket chirps, which coincided with the temperature, were faster than normal. She made it a habit to count them as a method of falling asleep each night. The chirps were off the past couple of nights, something common prior to a big storm. Was a big weather event about to occur? She had read that birds perch more before a storm because the air pressure is lower. Those at lower pressures eat more – anticipating a rough flight – and those in high pressure eat less and are more active. If weather were the factor, it would explain a lot of things. But birds were also less active long before the occurrence of an earthquake, which she had noticed prior to the one that led to the collapse of UL-One.

Of the hundreds of pages she had read on meteorology from her slate and from books Carter had given her, she began to focus in on bioclimatology—the effect of climate on human behavior. Humans of every culture had written tomes on the subject going back thousands of years. She focused her memory on the aspect regarding high winds. When wind of velocity interfaced with sand, snow, and possibly even water, the friction created positive ions at the surface. One theory held that somehow the ions reached the jet streams to travel faster than the storm front.

Animal systems reacted to positive ions, which probably included birds, cicadas, crickets, dogs, young children, and adults who paid attention to such climatic events. The latter included herself. She surmised it might include Jay and Wei, as well.

Hurricane season had begun, a real problem, which meant little in the rearrangement of today's new world, yet, everything considered, bespoke of a very large incoming storm. She woke her sleeping husband and explained her thinking and her conclusions.

"When do you think it'll come in?" he inquired, propped up on a pillow.

"Maybe a week or less. Before you say we've been through storms before, let me say this. The greenhouses won't be able to withstand objects flying through them. We could be down for months. We need to build a windbreak for both of them. We're only 340 miles from the coast. We could get hit with one of those Category 5 or 6 hurricanes and those reach maybe 600 miles inland."

Carter calculated, "With windbreaks, all together, you're probably looking at walls totaling maybe 500 square feet. We don't have the bricks to do it, not here or in Sedona. To do more building we'd have to find more brick yards. Too bad we don't have enough panels. Wait, actually, we do have a two left over from the enlargement of the residence hall to take care of one of the greenhouses. It would give us 30-feet-by-8 feet, well, 7 ½ feet, once it's set into concrete. We need two more. Unfortunately, the rest are buried under a hundred tons of rubble in UL-One."

Jess exclaimed, "I know where we can get two

more." Before Carter could say a word, she said, "From the pass. We collect the two we put boulders on, the ones still covering the Big Hole and the cluster of other holes. It's a logistical issue. We need the U-Haul to pick up two panels. There's no other way to bring them back, I mean they're too big to tie on to the roof of a car. The problem is, you don't drive over there, pick them up, and come home because there is no way to turn around the truck until you're completely over the pass and down in the desert again."

Carter completed the explanation. "Then you drive back over the panels, stop and retrieve them, load them, and come home. Total travel time maybe 10 hours, if you're lucky."

He chuckled, "Count Ken out. He never wants to see the pass again. I'll get Gregor to pick someone to partner with him. They can leave first thing in the morning."

Jess said, "I'll make a general announcement at breakfast about our plans."

Carter added, "I'll get crews to start digging two narrow trenches 30 feet in length and get enough quick-set concrete ready to pour into them when the panels arrive. Keep your fingers crossed the weather stays warm at least until the new walls are secure."

"Where's Gregor, I need him," Carter said, collaring Ken who had emerged from the meeting hall, having finished breakfast.

"I sent him to Cottonwood for some car parts. He

won't be back 'till early this afternoon," Ken said. "What do you need him for?"

"He's one of the few who has the skill to drive the U-Haul over the pass," Carter answered.

"Well, you know I'm not doing it. Besides, I'm teaching advanced auto mechanics this afternoon," Ken announced. "Which leaves you."

Carter complained, "I can't go. I have to supervise the ditches. If they're not perfectly straight, the panels won't fit into them."

"Then you'll have to wait until he gets back," Ken concluded.

By 2:00 p.m., Gregor gassed the truck and took A.J. along for the ride. At 8:30 p.m. Ken got a call at home on the sat phone, spoke for some time and came over to Carter, who had two wriggling babies and a dog on top of him.

"What?" Carter asked, annoyed.

Ken said, "Gregor called. He said the panels are loaded, but he's stuck. Fuel line got loose."

"So, he's a good mechanic. Tell him to fix it," Carter replied, not hiding the frustration in his voice.

"He can't. He said you borrowed the tools from the U-Haul the other day to fix your Mercedes and never returned them."

"Damn. Guess I'll have to bring him the tools," Carter moaned.

"There's more," Ken added, frowning.

Carter gave Ken a quizzical look. Jay and Wei stopped tinkering with their electronics and Jess stopped reading to listen. A family had few secrets.

"Take a car you're willing to lose," Ken said.

"Huh?"

"Jay, explain it to him. You might have to spell it out, because he's not too bright," Ken suggested.

Jay took a breath before telling Carter something he didn't need to hear. "You're going to drive up there at night. The vehicle you take will come nose-to-nose with the U-Haul. You will fix the problem, which presents another problem. How are you going to return in the car you took, because there is no room to turn around there? What are you going to do, back up in pitch darkness around mountain curves up and down hills for miles?"

"Oh, shit," Carter finally got the broad picture. Whatever vehicle he chose would have to be sacrificed and shoved off the cliff once the U-Haul got repaired to enable the truck to return the two panels to the compound. There was no other way. Of all the vehicles in the compound, a single one stood out that must be sacrificed: his beloved Mercedes, the one he had used to pick up his wife on their first date.

Carter took a few moments to gather several things, including water and food for the stranded men, said good-by to his wife, children, and dog, and began to walk out the door. He stopped and turned to say, "In my next life, I want to be a dog in good home."

Ken replied, "Maybe you already were and you screwed up somehow and got turned into a human as punishment. And here you are."

Carter didn't know whether to laugh or ignore

the statement until Ken said, "Don't forget to take the tools."

Carter flipped him off and closed the door behind him.

The long drive gave Carter time to think of Jess's problem and the answer came to him. Dehydration. Of course. The outside temperature didn't matter. A person still needed to drink plenty of water, otherwise one of the first indications of dehydration would be headaches. And some people needed more than others. Plain and simple.

He also thought about the challenging world his children had inherited, one in which multiple skills must be learned and to become as educated as possible, if they hoped to survive with no feel whatsoever of the world before.

Tabula rasa, a blank slate, he thought. A concept developed by the 17th Century philosopher, John Locke, who proposed that babies are born almost vacuous, and that all knowledge is gained by learning, experience, and perception.

Would he be around to see his children mature into adults? He had his own demons. It wasn't like the old days when he and Ken and maybe Beth would come up here to construct a house. He couldn't help but place the welfare and survival of the community on his shoulders, which left him little time for himself to deal with his own demons.

Approaching midnight, Carter nosed up to the U-Haul and got out. He had the flagrant idea that he might bypass the big truck and do as it did, drive down into the desert and come back. On closer inspection, he saw the big truck stood in the center of the roadway leaving insufficient room to pass it on either side. Nor could it maneuver out of the way enough for him to pass, even when the panels were laid down again. These days it was one car one way. It seemed like the simplest thing turned out to be a major project.

With the Mercedes' lights on, Carter had a clearer view of the east-west split running across the highway, now that the panels did not cover it. The original split was perhaps eight to ten feet which one panel easily covered to permit a vehicle to pass over it. Over time, the split had widened so much beneath the panel it barely covered it. In addition, the other panel failed to cover the numerous array of enlarging potholes creeping out along its edges. If boulders had not been placed on both of them, they would have been blown into the chasm below to disappear forever. In another few weeks, the roadway would be gone completely. The pass would be impassable.

A half-hour after Carter's arrival, repairs to the U-Haul were completed with the battery of the truck providing power to a drop-light rigged beneath the hood assisted by the headlights of the Mercedes. Gregor returned the tool box to the area behind the driver's seat in the truck where it belonged and started the engine. It ran perfectly. A.J. slammed the hood down and Carter walked over to the driver's window of the truck and said to Gregor, "Right now we're on flat ground. I want you to get into the car and turn the wheels hard to the right, release the emergency brake, shift into neutral, and get out. I'll do the rest."

A.J. said, "Carter, we know how much this hurts. Let me do this for you."

Carter looked at the young man. He might as well be talking to his father, an older twin in charge of medicine. Yet, here was the doctor's son, trying to ease the suffering of another over the loss of a mechanical device. "Thank you, A.J. I'll never forget your offer, but this is something I have to do."

Changing places with Gregor, Carter waited for him to do as instructed. When Gregor returned to the passenger seat in the truck, Carter put it in gear and inched up to the Mercedes, hit the bumper and slowly pushed the car. It arched to the left until the rear wheels were at the edge of the precipice, then continued to push until the Mercedes gave up all hope of survival and began its plunge into the dark depths.

Before it hit bottom, Carter hit the gas and drove ahead in the black night as fast he might, in an effort to save their city, trying to block out what just happened. Nothing about this felt right, nor did conditions portend improvement.

4

Jess had the timing wrong. The insects and animals weren't responding to a developing hurricane in the Pacific Ocean, the creatures were responding to a new series of micro-tremors growing in size. The San Andreas Fault had long ago unzipped from the Gulf of Mexico through the Salton Sea and up through California to flood the new watercourse when the western portion of California split off from the rest of the continent. It lay as an island sliver unto itself, perhaps destined to be a tourist mecca in future centuries.

The massive influx of water from the Gulf of California pulled water from the Pacific Ocean. Along with the redistribution of water on the planet and the subsequent effect on Earth's wobble, an additional stain was put on the major tectonic plates and their hundreds of tributaries.

The Pacific Plate and the North American Plate returned to sliding past one another, even after the

Big One had occurred only a few years earlier to release energy pent up for some 30 million years. Quakes of lesser magnitude rippled along hundreds of other fracture lines northeast into northern Arizona and Sedona, areas that possessed their own share of weakened faults.

The quake could not be considered enormous. It carried enough energy to cause a rattling of the compound, the barking of dogs, and the partial collapse of two greenhouses. If the wind turbines had not been securely anchored, they, too, might have collapsed. No other areas of Sekah City displayed damaged to any significant degree.

However, a husband and wife team had finished their breakfast early and walked the few steps to the greenhouse attached on one side to the meeting hall in order to begin their shift. After less than a half hour, the earthquake hit. One of the arch supports that held the polyethylene sheeting on top broke loose and struck the husband in the forehead, which caused him to fall and strike the back of his head on the concrete floor. The normally strong breeze got underneath the sheeting, caught it, and blew it loose from its ties. The capsid panels used for the walls and the newly installed windscreen remained intact.

The husband got killed, either by the initial blow, or by the fall, although he complained of stomach pains the night before. The wife escaped with no injuries. His earlier complaints triggered renewed fear that another killer might be on the loose and Alex sought permission from the wife to conduct an autopsy to determine the cause of death. Jess's opportunity had arrived.

At the first rumblings, Carter and other breakfast goers ran outside to get away from any structures only to watch the damage to the greenhouse and see the accident occur. All of them wondered about other damage to their community and Carter took it personally. He had used the last four remaining precious panels as windbreaks for something that had never occurred and lost his precious Mercedes for no reason.

He contemplated the enormous the task of breaking them out of the concrete for storage. However, hand-chiseling a total of 60 linear feet of concrete down half a foot to remove the four panels did not sound like an inviting task to attract joyous volunteers.

Jess, Alex, and A.J. transported the body to the small veterinary building in Sedona, dubbed The Hospital, a non-descript structure outfitted with a single aluminum adjustable height operating table provided by Carter and Jess. With Alex as a guide, Jess, and A.J. delicately butchered the husband in their quest for truth. The area on his forehead where the arch support had struck did not appear to be other than a large split in the skin. The stomach contents revealed an abnormally high number of partially digested jalapeno peppers. The medical report noted that witches were not at fault for his demise, but overeating his favorite foodstuffs most likely played a role in his complaints.

Jess had the idea that the surgeons might as well check his heart, liver, and kidneys to ensure they were in proper condition prior to his death. Finally, the enthused medical staff thought to check the back of the man's head where a large dent gave them the answer. Death by concussion. This information would be duly noted by the surgical team to be a part of his records. The first "complete" autopsy had been performed.

Working alongside Jess, Alex and A.J. found her knowledge to be profound, her memory of the intricacies of anatomy she had read and studied coming to the fore. After her first incision with the scalpel, her natural feel for the blade and her use of clamps clearly exceeded theirs.

Now that the Bailey episode had ended Jess spent all her available time studying medicine, reading copiously, and learning at a rapid pace. A small part of her effort was for Danny, the remainder for herself. She assisted in the repair of broken arms and various sprains, suturing cuts, and secretly wishing for a death so she might delve into the innards of the corpse.

In her moment, Jess fell into the groove, the same hunger that boiled in those who preceded her, those whom she had read about, adored, and wanted to emulate. She felt herself one of them, yearning for infinite knowledge, allowing the river of desire and knowledge to sweep her into its arms and to sculpt her into whatever it wanted. She felt herself suctioned into a completely alien concept, as though all she had ever done had prepared her for this signal moment of thought, of realization. She wanted to be a doctor.

Something instantly changed in her perception of herself and the world. Nothing about it frightened her. She had found her majesty. In fact, it excited her far beyond any feeling she had ever experienced. She wanted to expand her embrace to encompass even those few who might submit to her ministrations. At the most, she must force herself to doctor the world, if necessary. She felt herself the embodiment of Pasteur, Koch, Curie, even Hippocrates himself. These feelings were so intense she wondered whether they were valid or part of some flashback from her recent drug-induced experiences.

She found herself casting all other experiences aside, finding little time for her husband and children.

Danny had told her she was a rare breed and must develop her skills before distractions pulled her away from her destiny. Taking Danny's words to heart, Jess disavowed her duties as mayor, mother, and wife to become obsessed beyond anything she had ever conceived of. She Jess drove herself into medicine to such an extent the small community became concerned for her welfare. She, in turn, became concerned about diagnosing every complaint to the nth degree, frequently in disapproval of the doctors who told her she tended to overlook the obvious.

Carter knew the remaining medical staff struggled, especially after the demise of Danny. As such, he believed he could only do one thing, accede to the doctors' wishes and provide them with the medical equipment they desperately needed to get more information from dead bodies. This necessitated a short trip up north.

He spoke to Jess about a day's outing. "Here's a thought. How about if we take a ride up to Flagstaff for something different to do? I already talked to Beth and she offered to watch the kids."

"Sounds fantastic. This place might operate more smoothly with us gone for the day," she answered, enthusiastically, using a sense of humor that Carter and Ken affected to deal with harsh events.

Carter drove the newest addition to the fleet, a windowed panel van while Carla lay between him and Jess.

Unbeknownst to Jess, Carter's first stop would be at Flagstaff General Hospital. The doctors had done a Class A-1 job in carving up Blondie, trying to read and learn as they went, acknowledging they needed equipment and experience. Equipment included more scalpels, a variety of blunt tip scissors, bone saw, rib shears, absorbent materials, another autopsy table, a good microscope, and a tape recorder. Wet dripping gloves did not mesh well with picking up a pencil to write notes.

Although Carter loved his wife dearly, he felt no need to share the doctors' requests with her. Once that happened, he knew she would revert to the human condition and would, forevermore, visualize Blondie, the women she had known all her life, as having been cut down the middle with her organs removed. He would do his best to avoid that.

A gust of wind hit the van and shook it, almost as a "Welcome to Flagstaff" declaration. At the same time, they passed a road marker that read 6100 FEET ELEVATION. Riding shotgun, Jess traced her finger along a map directing Carter toward the first hospital. He slowed suddenly to avoid hitting a pack of six feral dogs of mixed breeds going in the opposite direction. He laughingly referred to them as a six-pack. To him, wildlife in general might be increasing in the surrounding Coconino National Forest, something to look forward to. Carla saw the dogs out the side window and barked, even after they were out of sight.

The long dead city was still partially covered in melting snow and ice, only some two thousand feet higher in altitude than Sedona. Jess shuddered at the desolation. Even the old Phoenix she knew had a few people and a couple of vehicles moving about. Somehow, the white bleakness made it seem more barren. She saw countless ghosts, each dressed in white, each with its own tale of woe.

Carter stopped the car in front of their destination. The granite facing on the building in front of them read FLAGSTAFF GENERAL HOSPITAL. Both had a strong remembrance of their previous visit to another dead hospital at Fort Huachuca military base in the southern part of the state near the Mexican border during their first date.

Walking around to the rear of the van, Carter opened the back door and grabbed a large empty satchel. "Babe, why don't you see what you can find for food stores. I'm going over to the surgical wing to pick up a few things the doctors want. Meet you back here in thirty."

Turning in her seat, Jess said, "Carla, you come with me." The dog wagged her tail in understanding.

A map on the interior wall of the five-story hospital guided them to their destinations. Jess headed downstairs, Carter went upstairs. Each carried a weapon and a radio. One face-off with a rabid dog and another with a murdering cave-dweller had taught Jess the necessity of being weaponized. Carter also wore a sat phone on his belt.

Lugging the heavy satchel to the car, Carter found Jess loading in a carton box filled with unopened boxes of instant mashed potatoes and a variety of spices. "What'ya got there, the kitchen sink?" she asked, seeing the weight of the bag he carried, as he leaned to one side.

Carter hefted the heavy bag back into the rear of the truck with a clunk of metal. If Ken had asked the question, he would have replied, "No, only a bone saw for cutting off limbs from dead, or possibly live, people; rib-cutting shears to split a person down the middle, a couple dozen pair of good neoprene gloves to root around in the guts of corpses, and a bunch of other goodies you don't want to know about."

Instead he replied, "Basic tools and supplies they wanted. That's all. I do need you to help me carry a table, though."

Once the adjustable-height aluminum table was loaded, Carter said, "Wait, hang on, one more thing." He returned minutes later carrying a box with a handle containing a Zeiss binocular microscope and boxes of slides, coverslips, and stains tucked inside. He carried a huge hard-cover tome titled *Human Pathology* under the other arm. When Jess saw this, she took the book from him and began to thumb through the table of contents, leaning against the van, flipping the book open to several sections, going back and forth, speed reading.

Carter took a seat on the front steps of the hospital and patiently waited fifteen minutes. Finally, he walked over to his wife and put his hand on the open book she held, saying gently, "Time to go, dear."

With the business part of the trip concluded, Jess took the wheel, heading for one of the residential areas of the city to see what could be found. There was no such thing as a true vacation by any of their people who left the compound. Finding valuables necessary for survival always reigned foremost in their minds.

Based on a variety of maps in their possession, Carter directed his wife to the wealthier section of the city. On the drive and in a moment of feeling forlorn, Jess said, "I miss home."

Carter reached over and patted Jess's leg gently, and said, "You belonged to a wonderful society. You had it all, save an abundance of sunlight." At that moment, Carla put her muzzle on the console between them to receive Jess's hand.

Swerving to miss a pothole, Jess reminisced. "Except the gossip got so stupid at times I wanted to scream. The prejudice against siders always bothered me. I never felt that way."

Carter looked out the window. He started to say something, but stopped himself. Jess caught it. "What?" she asked.

"Nothing, honey, a private thought."

"Do you want to share it? I won't tell. Carla won't, either, will you dear?" She scratched Carla's head, teasing.

Carter looked at her hard. "It's good you feel that way about them. I mean, do you love me and trust me and that we share this life as though we're twins?"

"What?" She immediately stopped the van in the middle of the street and turned off the engine, wondering if he had found another woman, or wanted a divorce, or perhaps he had terminal cancer. Taking a deep breath and looking him in the eyes, she said "All right, I'm listening."

"You read a lot don't you?" He asked.

"What does that have to do with anything?"

"Answer the question," Carter pressed.

"Yes, when I can. I used to read a lot more," she replied, wondering where this was going.

"What did you read?"

"Tolstoy, Christie, Huxley, Bradbury, Stevenson,

DeCarte, Aristotle . . . too many I can't remember."

"Yes, you can. If you really put your mind to it, I'll bet you can remember absolutely everything you ever read. Don't answer me. Do it."

Jess fell silent for several moments while her mental registry flipped through the cards on file. She finally replied, "Let's say it is true. What's your point?"

"You'd better have a long talk with your mother about when you were conceived and when the virus ravaged the planet. You may want to recall the part in Dustin Jones' diary where he talks about mutants and then talk to Jay and Wei. Because, love of my life, I am so happy you have nothing against siders, because I believe you are one."

5

Jess stared at him for a brief moment and began to laugh so hard that Carla began to bark, while Carter sat solidly in place watching tears flow down her face. At last, she caught her breath, put both palms to her face to wipe off the tears, and said, "Oh, sweetheart. Thank you. I needed that."

Carter looked at her, his face as emotionless as a rock carving, until she recovered enough to say, "You are serious, aren't you?"

"Yes."

Wondering about her husband's naïveté, Jess said, "Honey, do my eyes and mouth look off-set, do my physical features match anything resembling those of a sider?"

"No, but your brain does. Even Randolph didn't know it, but 'there are mutants, and then there are mutants'. That's a quote from Dustin. Didn't you ever wonder how you sailed through your second visit here when you came with James? Or about your memory, or your ability to learn so fast, or your high grades?"

"But I got the influenza and brought it back to UL-One?" she cried. "People died."

"Nobody said siders weren't human-—well, maybe a few—but they are. Dustin believed that, while there were physical deformities to go along with increased mental acuity, brain power can increase without the deformities. He gave several examples of it. A small window occurred during the fertility-infection period where this occurred."

"So?"

"So nothing. I'm saying I think you're one of those, that's all. Talk to Jay and Wei. See what they think."

"But I've done some pretty dumb things," she complained.

"Honey, high intelligence has absolutely nothing to do with making occasional bad decisions."

"Carter, that means our babies are part sider, too," she exclaimed.

"And?"

Jess remained silent, thinking. If she were a sider, so what? The virus made humans and animals more intelligent after infection and caused siders to be even more intelligent than the average person which included a faster rate of learning. What would others in the community think of her? No, that's old school. Nobody cared anymore, did they?

Looking for a random home to pull in front of in the exclusive Lindberg Springs portion of town, she saw one that attracted her interest. Waist-high weeds had overgrown the front. The two-story home was constructed entirely of tree logs, with a wrap-around deck. The three emerged from the car and seconds instant later Carter forced open the front door to find marble flooring throughout, with a wooden staircase and interior walls of stone. A large chandelier attached to the ceiling some 20 feet above them graced the open space of the great room.

Jess stood still and stared, marveling at the opulence, from the furnishings to the wall hangings. Carter directed Carla to look for people and when she returned, having found none, they searched the five-bedroom six-bath home and finally collected a quality knife sharpening stone as the single useful item.

Short minutes later, Jess drove up a long street that turned out to be a driveway with its own street name. It culminated at an 8,000 square-foot three-story wooden mansion set back 50 feet from the circular driveway. Weather had beaten away the varnish with indications that termites still enjoyed working on the multi-million dollar residence. A small spring-fed lake with forest on three sides could be seen from the front yard. A broken boathouse and collapsed pier served to remind visitors to beware. Nature owns this property.

Again, Carter forced open the door only to be assailed by a solid wall of stink. Both stared at what lay in front of them. Carla whined and Jess began rubbing her irritated eyes from odors consisting of

moldering materials, fragranced products, undefined chemicals, and whatever creatures of the night
brought with them during their stay in the dwelling.
In another life, an indoor air quality specialist would
bring back instruments to monitor the air and to
write scientific reports on the findings.

"Hoarders," Carter declared.

"What's that?" Jess inquired.

"They're people who won't stop buying and collecting things," he explained. "Nothing ever gets
thrown away, not pill bottles, not old TV sets, not
empty jars. Some people collected stamps or coins
or cars. These people collected everything. We've
got a house that has been locked up like this for decades.

"Back in Texas, I once knew a family that hoard-
ed food. They purchased extra refrigerators and
freezers in case they had to survive by themselves
for a long period of time. Predicting the electricity might fail during such an emergency, they also
bought boxes and cans of food. They had a hoarding
disease. I read once that some 10 percent of Americans were hoarders."

Trying to breathe shallowly, the couple made a
quick exploration of the home while Carla marked
territory at her own whim, which seemed to be frequent. Before them, rows of newspapers and magazines were stacked to the ceiling, clothing lay in
piles everywhere on the floor and stairway, used
dishes lay unwashed in the sink and stacked onto
the stove, pizza boxes and fast food wrappers were

strewn about randomly, the seven bedrooms and six bathrooms were almost impossible to navigate. Flower pots stood in the bathtubs, bathroom sinks, and on top of the commodes. One wall in the master bedroom was devoted to award photographs of an Olympic track and field start replete with a collection of gold and silver medals along with signed pictures of a man standing with the President and other team members holding an American flag.

"It's a sickness, Jess, or at least it used to be. It didn't matter whether you were rich or poor. People in trailers did the same thing."

Seeing so many material goods in one place did not surprise Carter, even in a home that size, but to Jess, who grew up in a city where a single room in this house could serve over 200 people, she could not convey in words the depth of the pain that tore at her soul.

"How do you cope with the insanity of this world, Carter?" She wanted to cry, to let it out, to scream, when she saw the terrible waste, trying to overcome nausea. Finding herself unable to take a deep breath, she said, "Please, let's get out of here."

Carter thought of saying something clever like, "Insanity is a relative term. The people who lived here would definitely say the same thing about where you used to live." He bit his tongue and thought before stepping on it. *Foot in mouth disease*. He told her, "I don't try to deal with it. A long time ago, I learned to accept what came along and not intellectualize about it. That make life less complicated. It's also bad karma to get too involved. It's like saying, 'what else could go wrong'? Things tend to go south when you do that."

Jess had lost her nerve. Any semblance of courage flew away on wings. "I'm done. Let's go, "she declared, and began to walk out the door. She'd had enough of civilization."Hold on a second." Carter said. He swiftly and carefully navigated his way across the spacious living room to the opposite wall, trying not to trip and break his neck. He pulled away a sofa piled high with clothing stacked on top of a large toaster oven. A moment later, having found the fireplace, he emerged carrying a poker, small hatchet, and an armload of logs, set them down, then said, "There might be something we can use. Go on out for some fresh air and I'll make a last tour."

A short while later he emerged from the home carrying a great discovery for their community: an armload of board games, all wrapped in cellophane and unopened. "There are more. Hold your breath if you have to," Carter emplored.

Overcoming her momentary panic attack, Jess assisted in gathering another 15 games, including 10 jigsaw puzzles, from 500 pieces to 2000 pieces. Of these, one lone exception stood out: an unopened six-pound box containing an 18,000 piece picture of Venice Italy to include its stores and residences, canals, oarsman, tourists, birds, and whatever complexities might be present to promote insanity and backaches. Carter remarked, "This is one you give to somebody you don't like. We might need to build a special room for this one. It'll be our version of a prison sentence."

Acknowledging their riches, Jess still had the urge to set the home on fire. She didn't see only thousands of materials goods. She saw a house filled with ghosts of people the goods once belong to. She saw waste that might have saved lives under other conditions and it disgusted her beyond measure. It also scared the hell out of her, triggering some un-defined response akin to evil that made her shudder. As a compromise to torching the home, she left the door wide open knowing that snow and rain would enter and not caring in the least. Let nature, the true property owner, finish off the mausoleum.

Jess got behind the wheel. Happy to be in her own territory, she started the car and sped away from the dark forces and the feeling of having wallowed in filth. A moment later, she said, "Honey, find me the library."

Within a short time, she pulled in front of the City of Flagstaff Public Library. The entire block that encompassed the building stood, unaffected, presumably because it abutted the county museum, both constructed of solid granite.

Jess did not expect to see much in the building, perhaps to find a particular piece of information. In her previous life, down below, hundreds of leath-er-bound volumes adorned their own library, which only went so far to serve a limited population over many years. The reading slates did offer an endless supply of reading material, but reading from plastic imprints never could convey the impact delivered by an actual hands-on book.

The building smacked of a special mustiness. Jess discovered that the odors introduced a new level of sensory challenges comprised of the myriad components of dirt combined with knowledge, all collected over time, incubated, and exhaled for her pleasure. She sensed an envelopment, as though she were being wrapped in a cocoon of protection, which served to drop her level of anxiety. Hundreds of thousands of books gave rise to this richness, all waiting to be read, many perhaps to be brought back to her city for the creation of their own library.

Once she finished reading what she came for, the three found a sheltered gazebo in which several signs were hung advising the public to ensure their community remained safe from careless fire usage. Jess thumbed through the pathology book Carter had recovered, which would complement the *Gray's Anatomy* she constantly studied while at the medical center.

6

Jess began rubbing her temples and her eyes to such an extent that Carter had to ask,

"Babe. Are you all right?"

"I will be in a minute," she responded.

"Maybe you're working too hard," he offered, trying to be helpful only to feel ridiculous. If hard work caused headaches, he and countless others would have been weeded out long ago.

"I said I'm all right," Jess shot, then immediately regretted her attack on her husband.

"No worries," Carter responded, hoping to end the conversation.

Carla caught two rabbits, which the couple added to the vegetable stir fry brought from home, ensuring enough rabbit remained for their provider to have her reward. The meal finally completed, a reanimated Jess asked, casually, trying to switch gears from angry housewife to fun vacation partner, "What's next on the to-do list?"

"I want to check out something, see what it looks like today, maybe get some ideas for a move I'd like most of us to make to Cottonwood," he said, this time taking the wheel to drive to a location only three miles away. He told her about the township of Cottonwood, located only 30 miles south of Sedona, a small community encompassing only a little over 10 square miles, still replete with Walmart and other big box stores. The Verde River ran through the area that lay waiting for those who had the courage to rebuild.

As Carter pulled into his next stop, Jess queried, "It looks like a city within a city. What is this place?" she asked.

"It was one of the largest truck stops in the country, the I-40 Truck Stop. It's got over a hundred pumps, a great hotel, a buffet restaurant and fast food eateries, movie theater, showers for truckers, and gift shops."

Stopping in front of the huge hotel, the three exited the vehicle. An inch of snow slush remained on the ground. A number of roofing tiles had flown in from somewhere, possibly from miles away, to shatter the glass, leaving fragments of red clay tiles littering the floor.

"There is no electricity, so the electronics will be off. Let's have a look," Carter offered, clearing out enough remaining glass to create a safe passage. We'll have to climb through because the automatic doors won't open. Everything else will be shut off, though, so we should be good.

"Carla, be careful of the broken glass," he directed.

With Carla close behind, the couple entered the building lobby and took a long hallway going from one conference room to another. "There are probably a dozen of these," he explained. Jess stood in each room, gasping at the enormity of each, with its colorful carpeting and ornate lighting fixtures. Leading her to the dining room and then into the huge kitchen, Jess could only shake her head from side to side, speechless.

Smiling, amused at her incredulity, he said, "Let's hit the stairs and check out the rooms."

The door to the first room swung open easily. Jess stared at the twin queen-sized beds, the large flat screen TV, nightstands, small refrigerator, microwave, and full bathroom, trying to comprehend it all. She walked over to the window and drew open the drapes to view the vast acreage of buildings and trucks parked below her. She had no questions to ask. Turning away from the window, she flopped onto one of the beds, declaring "Oh, this smells musty like the small ones we slept in down in Fort Huachuca. How many rooms are there in this place?"

"Probably around 200," he answered. Grinning broadly, he said, "Get up a second." She did, and he pulled off the top cover, throwing it onto the floor. "Lay down again," he directed, with tease in his voice. She did so, and he lay down beside her with Carla relaxing on the floor next to them, watching, protecting.

An hour later, they dressed and returned to the car to explore the dimensions of the theater. Both mused at Jess's recollection of the time not long before when she and James had visited a small, hot room with a torn screen on her second visit to Phoenix.

From the theater, the trio took a slow trip to the main restaurant and the kitchen that once served 24-hour buffets for travelers using U.S. I-40 to cross the country.

"Baby, we could move everybody here and live like kings," Jess fanaticized.

Carter said nothing. He had already told her about how electricity was once supplied to all of Flagstaff had originated from a coal-fired plant located in Holbrook, 90 miles to the east. With nobody to work the plant, let alone provide the coal, and with lines and roads down everywhere, power for their needs could be counted out. Plus, water pumps required electricity and all the mains were ruptured. In summary, they had no chance of providing enough power and water for a mass of people located in a single hotel for drinking, cooking, bathing, washing and flushing.

"How about this for an idea?" Carter said. "We take our folks up here for a day's outing in the school bus. We might need to do it over a couple of trips. Only a handful of your people lived in a big city before moving to UL-One." Immediately after saying those words, he chided himself for his lapse of judgment. Even intelligent people can say dumb things.

"To what end?" she asked, not happy with his idea.

Carter knew what his wife wanted to say—that exposing others to what she had seen and felt could only cause pain; knowing what they had lost out on, what they never had, nor would ever have, what others lost and wasted in a world devoid of civilization. No good would come of it. In fact, if he really wanted to cause pain, he could tell her cruel, hard facts about how humans lived and the actual amount of world-wide waste of food and resources.

Leaving the hotel, Jess made a U-turn and drove slowly at Carter's direction, making a right turn, until some 50 yards from their destination, Carter held up his hand. "Stop," he ordered. She did. He took his rifle from between them and exited the car. "Stay here and follow my hand signals," he said quietly, slowly and gently closing the door.

Jess placed her hand on the rifle immediately to her right. She knew the tone of voice he used meant possible trouble in the offing. She saw her husband walk forward while staring at the ground, looking around, and moving forward all the time. Some 10 yards from the building, he turned to Jess, made a slashing motion across his throat, put a finger to his lips, and waved her forward.

Jess killed the engine and exited the truck, leaving the door partially open to avoid the noise of closing it. She moved cautiously toward Carter.

Carla, sensing her master's danger, listened to her instructions and followed her master who stood on a wooden walkway fronting the building. "Tire tracks," he explained, close to her ear, almost whispering. Pointing, he said, "Look at the dimensions of the grooves and how far apart they are. They're not made by a car like my Mercedes or some SUV, more like a heavier vehicle, maybe a military-type truck. See the broad, flat tracks? I'm not sure what those are. And look at the footprints coming and going. There are several sets of them. See the tread prints in the snow? Those are boot prints, not sneakers."

Jess watched and learned. "But it looks like they're gone, right?"

"Maybe some of them," Carter replied, quietly. They stood to the side of the truck stop restaurant where the glass front opened onto the gas pumps and likely, would not have been seen. The sky quickly darkened and heavy drops of rain began to fall.

To Jess, this was not a search and destroy mission, only one that required information without revealing any of their own. The situation was complex for Carla to understand. Jess needed to communicate to her a message entailing the search for people while running into and out of a building. Carla listened to Jess's instructions and followed them without incident.

"It's our turn." Carter directed, leading his assault team, such as it was, with weapons drawn, to enter an empty building through an unlocked door. The entry opened onto the buffet with ample seating at tables and counters. A large gift shop stood to their left with sleeping bags, full and empty liquor bottles, and other evidence of human occupation.

Continuing to move forward found them in the kitchen, although not the size of the one in the hotel, this kitchen still demanded respect. The area contained a four-burner stove made for cans of alcohol-jelly Sterno that was set onto one of two-eight burner built-in griddles. Coffee grounds lay atop other debris in a large metal trash can and a half a pot of warm stew still stood on the smaller stove.

Once, when Jess asked why Ken and Carter were happy *not* to find others, Ken told her, "Anybody we find will have survived for 20 years, like us. Survivors didn't fly in here for a happy weekend vacation to look at the colored rocks or pretty snowflakes. You're not going to live very long in this world without good weapons, a lot of ammunition, and a lot of smarts. Yes, we can get better weapons and a lot more ammo, but the point is, you don't survive by being friendly and opening your house to strangers. If you do, you could lose your house and your life. I didn't make up the rules for survival, nature did. In a word, if we see signs of people, we'd better be scared. I honestly don't know how to secure our community enough to keep out armed intruders, do you?"

Carter sternly admonished her, "Don't tell anybody about what we found here except for Ken, Jay, Wei, and Gregor. Ken will tell Beth. That's it. Hopefully, it'll rain enough to wash out our tire tracks."

Jess understood the severity of the situation. If word got out about others in their vicinity, possibly military types, a lot could go wrong. It seemed like the appropriate time to return home.

The couple quickly walked back to truck and this time Carter drove, in a hurry to get away but not enough in a rush to get into a one vehicle accident.

Once back in the compound, Carter drove the van up to the meeting hall where he dropped off the boxes of board games, and Jess went straight to Jay. Carter then drove the quarter mile to the medical center to deliver the new equipment he had retrieved from the hospital.

Jess found Jay working a cleanup shift in the yard to report on their findings in the restaurant. She had a sense of reticence about relating what Carter had told her about the possibility of her being a sider, not knowing how she would react to what he might tell her.

Jay said, "If you were conceived in UL-One and both your parents had the vaccine, then you would not have the deformities the rest of us have. Dustin Jones noted in his diary that the vaccine wasn't perfect. He believed there could be such a thing as a trace of infection whereby only part of the DNA is tied up, which, in your case, means the part controlling number and proximity of neurons and not the parts affecting the structural changes. So I'm not surprised at all at your intelligence, your memory, and your comprehension. If you accept that you are a sider, you'll lose a lot of self-imposed barriers and your rate of learning will increase significantly. Does that help?"

"It makes me feel unique," she replied. In truth, she had mixed feelings, from being prideful about belonging to an elite group, to being the subject of ridicule, to wanting to test out her new superpowers, as she fancifully considered them when they belonged to true siders.

7

Three days later and anxious to find out about progress Jay and Wei had made regarding the inhabitants of the truck stop, Carter found the couple working on another fish net upstream from the original one.

The three sat on the dirt of the river bank 100 yards from the bridge leading across the rapidly moving water. The compound lay them 200 yards behind them. Riki, Carla's litter mate, accompanied the trio. The day was overcast and gloomy, yet surprisingly warm. The fish screen lay on the gravel of the river bank. Snipping off short pieces of metal strapping Jay had acquired from the barn, the couple began to reinforce the attachment of the net to the screen.

Wei said, "We got smart and checked to see if there was any place that actually made drones, like you did when you got the AirStream mobile homes. Bingo."

"You'd still need line of sight, wouldn't you?" Carter asked.

Wei replied, "Pretty much. With the right transmitter and receiver, we can go from about 1.5 to 3 miles away from our base of operations. No problem watching the restaurant. We can't get to altitude with our little one, so we're hoping to find a larger drone for more wind stability. Once we find others, we can invite them to live with us. Right?"

Carter caught the sarcasm. "Right. Nobody said they're bad guys. They could be teachers who covet our school bus." He got up and dusted off his pants. "Okay, the sooner the better. Take the van. Make plans to stay for a week or two. When can you leave?"

"How's tomorrow," Jay asked. "We'll take Riki."

Working on the engine of the school bus three days later, Carter received a call on his sat phone from Jay, who said, "Thanks for the recommendation on the hotel, Carter, although it is a little above our pay grade. Right off, we found what we were looking for, a nice three-foot-diameter four-bladed drone along with what we needed to charge it off the car battery. We parked behind the loading dock at the hotel rear to hide the car and put everything together in the room."

Wei continued the tale. "The weather cooperated and we were able to get up to about 300 feet. We made quick flights over and around the hotel three times daily and recorded what we saw on the monitor. You were right. It's a military type truck."

Gregor looked at Carter, not understanding the conversation when Carter responded, "I thought about it and I'm guessing it's a half-track with regular wheels in the front and tracks in the back to enable it to maneuver like a car, but to go cross country. It's perfect for this environment. It can hold up to a dozen men. How many guys did you see?"

Wei said, "Five, as far as we could tell, all have either handguns or rifles."

"Can you describe any of them?" Carter inquired.

She and Jay did their best until Gregor, paying close attention to the conversation, announced, "That sounds like the one I hit at the caves. I mean, it was raining and it was a long shot, but I know I hit him in the right leg before he got away with some of his buddies. It's obvious, because there aren't too many people who are very tall, skinny, bald, and limping off the right leg like you're describing."

"Fucking cavers. There has to be more of them, otherwise, why all the weapons? Could you see any kind of routine they stuck to?" Carter asked.

"We're starting to get a general picture, but we'll need more time," Jay responded.

Ten days later, Jay called again. "Okay, here it is. All five would leave mid-morning on Mondays, drive somewhere out of range of the drone's camera, and return on Wednesday night, leave Thursday morning about 10:00, return by noon, sometimes with supplies, sometimes not, then repeat it again on Monday and Thursday. This is Sunday, so we expect them back tomorrow afternoon.

"What kind of supplies?" Gregor asked.

Jay answered, "Couldn't tell for sure, but it looked like small or large sacks of something they either hand-carried or slung over their shoulders. Sometimes they brought things in boxes."

"If they are cavers, they know we're here. They're very bad people. They have no remorse whatsoever. They're like Brendas and Baileys with guns. We need to go inside and do more exploring when they're gone. "You say you can range out to about three miles?"

"At most, from the camera to the receiver, but the camera itself is excellent. From altitude we could see out much farther out. They consistently go to the east and return from the east," Wei said.

Carter grinned. "I have an idea. It shouldn't put any of us in danger of getting shot. However, with my idea, there's a much greater chance we will get burned at the stake here at home than getting shot over there. For this to work, we'll need to move quickly. We don't want these guys to disappear on us. Keep watching and we'll try to be there by Wednesday or Thursday morning at the latest. Keep me informed if anything changes. In the meantime, I need to have a long talk with my wife."

8

Carter knew he had subjected his personal family to a terrible risk by asking Jess to find more devil mushrooms in the woods. He had asked her to prepare a brew similar to the same poison that had been used against them in their own food. If she were caught making this potion, a revolution would likely ensue and their death would be imminent at the hands of their own people. The sticking point: where to prepare the potion, because only a few knew there were any other people alive, let alone cavers who might be planning to take over their city. Jess couldn't prepare it at home because, even though Ken had told Beth in secrecy, Annie and Gregor frequently walked in unannounced. He didn't want either of them involved in this part of the operation.

If something went wrong, well, doubtless, survivors of the onslaught had not forgotten the humiliation they had received during a stormy night when virtually all their crew lost their lives while enjoying the warmth of their caves.

Ironically, the clandestine team chose the most secretive site of all—one already set up for the production of insanity and death—the barn loft.

The strangest of feelings overcame Jess. A few hours of work in the morning rewarded her with the mushrooms she sought. That was the easy part. Bringing them to the loft to process them as Brenda had done made her feel as though she were Brenda in Jess's body, preparing a brew to cause harm and suffering. She kept reminding herself that Brenda had done it for sport born out of sickness and her own purpose transcended that. This wasn't like her old closed community where somebody would be punished by putting them in Room 7 for a day or two for rehab. She faced outsiders who were bent on their elimination. By the time she finished extracting all she could out of the batch of mushrooms she had carefully selected, she felt very comfortable with herself.

During mid-day with the half-track still present, Carter and Ken drove in to the truck stop from a different direction and parked in the rear of the hotel out of sight down the loading ramp next to Jay's car. The two men emerged to enter the building from a rear door, which Jay had previously forced open.

Jay and Wei prepped the drone, while Ken and Carter went over the simple plan again, looking for small flaws in their thinking, obscure about things that might go wrong, discussing contingencies in each instance. The drone would serve as a lookout. If it were seen, Jay would radio the men. Their arrival prior to the departure of the cavers was calculated to be an insurance plan, in the eventuality all five, and not two or three, had left the premises.

That turned out to be the case, as five men climbed aboard the vehicle, making no attempt to lock the door behind them, and headed east, as the high flying drone revealed on the monitor. Nor did it observe any vehicle at the rear of the restaurant.

Carter drove the long way around and pulled into the loading bay at the restaurant's rear with a door set next to it, similar to the one at the hotel. On this side, no windows looked out onto the rear parking area. Once out of the truck, with crowbar in hand, Ken first gently pushed on the rear door of the restaurant and found it to be unlocked.

Riki received her instructions, ran in, and some moments later, ran out again as Ken held the door open during her excursion. She gave no growl, no indication that caution might be obtained. The snow had melted, tracks of their previous visit washed out, all to the good fortune of the intruders.

The men cautiously entered to find both small and large sacks of produce. First things first. Moving further into the kitchen itself, Carter's suspicions proved to be correct. To the great misfortune of the occupants, their eating habits came back to bite them. Their cook had prepared a large pot of vegetable stew with what appeared to be rabbit, ate it for lunch, and finished it for dinner. Without spilling a drop, he added the poison from the 4-ounce glass container of concentrate Jess had given him and stirred it into the stew with the wooden ladle still in the warm pot.

The visit to the restaurant lasted less than 60 seconds from entry to exit, until the men drove away to the safety of the hotel to await the evening and the arrival of their arch enemies. It went without saying anybody who had access to a military half-track could also have access to serious weapons.

At twilight, Wei sent up the drone, again from the rear of the hotel, only to find the men had arrived early. She brought it back, ensured it had a full charged, and waited an hour until the sound of gun shots charged Wei into action. She rocketed the drone skyward to its destination and the group watched the monitor. The tall, thin man came running-limping out of the restaurant, running to the right along the boardwalk, holding his side, with another man wearing overalls and a baseball cap following, hunched over, shooting at him. The tall, thin man arched his back and went down. A third man came out of the building with gun in hand shooting at apparent imaginary targets, until the man with the cap turned to shoot him several times.

The man with the cap saw the drone only yards away. Wei dove in on him, flying it in dizzying arcs around him like an angry wasp. He tried to follow it and within seconds, fell to the ground, pulled his knees to his chest, straightened them, and lay still.

"Get closer," Carter said. She did. The monitor depicted the man with the hat and handgun about Carter's age, but unshaved and weather-beaten. Life had not been good to him. He wore overalls with a wild-gray hair sticking out from beneath the cap.

"Wei, get closer," Carte requested, his face inches from the monitor. Immediately, he saw a diamond stud in one ear exposed to the camera. Carter exclaimed, "I know the son-of-a-bitch. Let me think. Yeah, back when I trained for the Rangers, he was one of the trainees. His name is Kody Davis, a real piece of work. We grew up in the same neighborhood and actually had it out. He was good fighter and a vengeful person and tried to jump me later on, but I beat him up pretty good a second time. Next thing you know, we're training together in the army and he's always giving me the stink eye.

"He got dishonorably discharged for selling drugs to the troops, their wives, and even their children. He got sentenced to ten years and got out in two. We were thinking somebody got paid off with some big money. Kody had deep connections and probably had a lot of money, possibly hooked in with the cartels. He hung with a nasty crowd after his dismissal. The guys in my group who made it through kept me informed. That was the last I heard of him. He's a legend. If he wasn't the leader of the bunch, I'd hate to see who is."

"Three down, two to go," said Ken.

An hour later, a night of pitch blackness began. Heavy clouds covered the moon. Not a star could be found. After Carter drove his big pickup to the rear of the restaurant and dropped off Ken and Riki, he drove to the front of the building to face the gift area where the men congregated, turned the headlights on bright, switched on all four roof-mounted spotlights and faced directly into the front of the building running right up onto the porch only feet from the window. At the same instant he gave two quick hits of the on-button of his radio which signaled Ken to release Riki in from the rear. Ken did so and followed her through the kitchen into the gift area. He heard shout of surprise, a single gunshot, followed by a snarl and a scream of terror. Ken saw one man on his back, his pant leg ripped open, a deep gash in his exposed thigh, Riki snarling, trying to go for the man's throat, ripping at the man's bleeding arms as he tried to protect himself. Ken shot the man twice, trying not to hit Riki or becoming blinded by the terrible light coming into the building from Carter's truck.

In a perfect example of timing, Carter came in the front door and saw the second man. Confused by the sudden action, the man tried to shield his eyes with one hand and shoot somebody, something, with the other. Carter shot three rounds into man's center mass, then emptied the remainder of the 12 round magazine into the body, almost before the man hit the floor.

Handoff from Jess to Ken, Carla, and Carter. All in the family.

"You sure you got him? Better check," remarked

Ken. His friend had hostilities that required venting on occasion, which made Ken thankful he was on their side.

The large front room smelled like alcohol, gunpowder, cooked food, sweat, and blood. Riki came over to Ken, wagging her tail, seeking and receiving a loving thank you. A hallucinating man is hardly a match for the intelligence and quickness of a large sider dog.

Seeing Ken unhurt, Carter pulled the radio from his belt and said, in terse sentences, "All over. Bring the van to the back. Let's load it up with these sacks in the back of the kitchen and get some sleep. Tomorrow, I want to find out where these guys got their supplies from." Grinning, he added "By the way, if you're hungry, I think there might be some leftover stew." He heard laughter at the other end.

Without saying a word, both men began to search the pockets of the five men for anything helpful. Only one of the five had anything of interest in their pockets. Kody Davis' right forearm was heavily wrapped in gauze and a flexible sports bandage with blood showing though. It appeared as though he had incurred a long deep gash, perhaps one that had not been stitched closed. The forearm was swollen and purple outside the bandage, indicating infection had set in.

In Kody's rear pocket Ken found a folded sheet of paper with a rough, but accurate, diagram of Sekah City. In his right front pocket he found a key ring with six keys, one of which probably fit their vehicle. The other keys might be for doors rather than cars. In his left front pocket Ken found a rare, beautifully cut three carat blue diamond mounted in a ring.

"The diamond is mine," Ken announced, holding it up.

Carter teased, "Correction. The diamond is Beth's, once you show it to her."

Based on the knowledge provided by Wei and Jay, Carter had drawn arcs from downtown to the east on a map of Flagstaff. Although the half-track had a maximum speed of 50 mph, the practical average speed would be more like 25-30 mph, due to fallen trees, obstructing vehicles, sink holes, and various detours. The times when the cavers had made a round trip in an hour, say from around 10:00 Thursday morning to Thursday noon, he surmised it might take them 15 or 20 minutes to get to their destination, which meant a travel distance of from six-to-ten miles. He reasoned the bunch had to spend time picking up groceries somewhere before returning. The two arcs he had drawn encompassed that range.

The next morning, Carter got behind the wheel of his truck and handed the map to Ken, explaining, "I made points on each sector two miles apart and connected them with zigzag lines to give us pie-shaped sectors. I numbered them. We'll take them one-by-one." Ken saw the area he had demarked, and passed the map back to Jay and Wei. Riki lay between them.

For obvious reasons, homes and office buildings did not fit into the scheme of things, which eliminated most of sectors one and two. This included a large burned out shopping center that may have been destroyed by a gas explosion based in the crater in the parking lot and the circle of debris around the old structures.

The team concentrated their efforts on finding some type of warehouse facility, either military-related, or perhaps a distribution center for a large box store, although the latter did not sell such sacks of products to the public at large. Jay thought to keep an eye out for a branch warehouse that shipped goods to other states or even to other countries via airports, or trucked the foodstuffs to the seacoast.

Nearly at the top peak of the triangle of the fourth sector, a large park stood before them untouched by human hands for decades and surrounded by ponderosa and lodgepole pine. The aspen in the center of the park were starting to leaf out. The occupants of the lone car in the lot emerged to find a concrete table nearby with concrete benches, which had no appeal to those who had been seated for hours.

In fact, the name of Flagstaff had originated from the fascinating story of the early explorations of the region by well-healed and multi-talented men named Leroux and Sitgreaves in the early 19th Century. Although there are several versions to the tale, the most popular has it that on July 4, 1876, another explorer of the territory stripped a lodgepole pine to its trunk and used it as a flagpole, hence the name *Flag-staff.*

With pine trees as a backdrop, Carter began to throw a stick for Riki to fetch, while thinking about his latest conversation with Jess regarding her headaches. "Baby, maybe you spend too much time at the microscope," he had mentioned, off-handedly.

"Sorry, my dear, unfortunately, no," she had returned. "There are two ways to get headaches from microscope usage. If too much light is projected from the bottom there is a possibility the brightness will cause a problem. As long as the rheostat is adjusted to the right dial setting, which mine is, that won't happen. Also, if the oculars are not set to the proper pupil distance, each eye will receive a different image. Mine are adjusted perfectly."

At the time, Carter felt mollified. "Sorry, not my area of expertise. Did you talk to the doctors about it?" he probed, doing his best to be a dutiful husband without pushing any hot buttons.

She replied, "I told them, yes. They asked me if was a migraine and told me migraines occur three times as frequently in women as men. I mentioned that it is an interesting coincidence that this form of headache occurs when a storm front is pending, trying to give them suggestions to a subject about which they had little knowledge, in my opinion."

Carter looked at his wife askance. *Does she think she's the king of the hill now?* No, she's simply condensing a previous conversation.

Jess wasn't finished. "Only Danny, the true doctor, seemed curious about my statement. He was about to ask me something when Alex wanted to know what part of the head hurt and did I have any food allergies and maybe I required more sleep. I said I didn't think any of that held in my case. Alex said peoples' perception of the cause of migraines is wrong 95% of the time and I told him I didn't suffer from migraines. Okay?"

Carter swung his head around in a circle, trying to keep up with his wife's presentation. He became even more concerned, after finding out his theory had no grounds. She had absolutely ruled it out, which reduced the problem down to the worst nightmare: a brain tumor. At what age do people get brain tumors? What else could it be? He wasn't a biologist. Maybe the doctors told her something terrible and she asked them not to tell anyone. Furthermore, he did not like her cavalier attitude. It's the same attitude he took when he suspected the worst of himself.

9

Jay pulled Carter out of his morbid thoughts, when he shouted, "What's that?" while pointing to the north. A single story, white structure stood a quarter-mile away, visible between the pines and not seen from their previous vantage point on the street.

"I don't know. Let's find out," Carter answered, happy to be distracted. Within minutes, he drove on a roadway that encircled the building measuring the size of a soccer field with street branches leading out from each direction. The west side of the building might have been a large parking area, now almost vacant, with the white striping washed away. A lone bullet-riddled Porsche stood out in the lot. Carter drove close to it and Ken got out to look.

"Skeleton inside." Then Ken stated the obvious. "These holes are from an automatic rifle, not a handgun," noting the way the holes clustered.

"Scarecrow," remarked Carter.

"What does that mean?" Wei asked from the back seat.

"If you saw that in your cornfield, would you want to land here?" Carter replied.

Continuing around the building in a counter-clockwise direction, Carter drove past a number of steel shipping containers stacked near the north wall. On the east stood two large hauler trucks, each carrying a container with every single wheel rim touching the ground.

"Hold on. I want to check out those trucks. You don't load until you're ready to ship," Ken suddenly announced.

Carter put on the brakes and everyone got out. Ken walked over to the first one—a large Mack flatbed with a standard steel shipping container on the bed that measured, 20' long x 8' wide and 8.5' tall. He easily slid into the cab of the truck now some 18" lower with the tires flattened, and announced, "Nobody home," while retrieving a clipboard with the shipping manifest. After only seconds of reading, he handed it to Carter, who appeared stunned and gave the list to Wei. She made a quick mental calculation and said, "Nearly 1400 cubic feet of goodies," and passed the manifest to Jay who said, "This is crazy, man."

Jay read out loud: "DELHI INDIA: 10,000 flexible-wrap bandages of varying sizes x 2; 10,000 bottles of mercurochrome, merthiolate, and Iodine x2; 1,000 bottles acetaminophen, oxycodone, hydrocodone, ibuprophen, naprosodium sulphate, and aspirin x 5 each, 500 bottles of multivitamins tablets x 10; 5000 tubes of toothpaste x 1; 10,000 toothbrushes x 2." He concluded by adding, "I guess it might have helped someone at some point in time."

In a moment of heavy thought, Ken replied, angrily and with rare venom, "Yeah, as if the people who needed it the most ever got more than a trickle, and all gone in a matter of days. And I'm not talking about only this shipment to India. Stuff like this goes directly to the black market and after administrators get their fair share, the price gets jacked up. The wealthy get richer and the poor people get the dregs. The good news is that we get the credit for being the good guys by donating all this and we get a UN vote in our favor from the country we gave the stuff to. Both sides rotten to the core, but what do I know?"

Ken went to the rear of the truck. Knuckling the steel of the container, he said to Carter, "There used to be 500,000,000 of these. That's a lot of steel." He grabbed one latch of the container, twisted it to a vertical position, and did the same with the other latch. He pulled open the doors to find cardboard and wooden crates with USDA stamped on each.

Ken closed the doors and headed toward the second truck, a double semi. The huge container on this one measured half again the length of the first one. He climbed into the cab to find another shipping manifest. With the door to the cab open, Carter could see him reading it, flipping from one page to the next, back and forth for a long time, until he heard Ken say, "Holy shit." He climbed out and handed the paperwork to Carter.

"What is it? I don't understand," Carter said, looking over the papers.

Ignoring him, Ken declared, "I don't believe it, "Iran? Fucking Iran?" he repeated. "You can't make this up. It's all coded, too. You know that I never have any expectations, but I never expected this. Besides me, there are few people left on the planet who understand these codes."

"There are only a few people left on the planet at all, as far as that goes." Carter looked up from reading the pages, confused at seeing his friend confused, and said, "Okay, talk."

Ken answered, "When I repaired planes for the air force, I knew most of the pilots on the base. One of them was my best friend. One day he explained in detail to me how to read this."

"You thinking what I'm thinking," Ken asked.

"Yep."

"There must have been another shipment, probably gone before that one. All those items won't fit in that one container."

"Nope."

"Ten crates of surface to air hand-held missile launchers."

"With 50 missiles."

"Ten 50 caliber truck-mounted machine guns."

"5000 rounds of 50 cal belted ammo."

"1000 Beretta M9 handguns plus ammo."

Carter said, "Interesting. That's the same kind we

use." For the benefit of Jay and Wei, he explained, "Back when I was in training, the subject of Iran came up. My CO told me about the huge military industrial complex in the country—monster might be a better word—and, except for nukes, the Iranians made everything, including handguns and drones to carry military grade explosives. This was all for 'national defense', which included heavily supporting terrorist organizations around the world. They didn't need our Berettas. What they needed was cash.

"With that in mind, the only one thing that makes sense to me is that all the cash money we gave got sunk back into American weapons. The American arms dealers were happy, the Iranians were happy because we paid for their weapons by giving them cash, and the terrorists were happy. If the insurgents got captured along with their weapons, the Americans would get blamed because our weapons were used. There would be a little mini-scandal about it in the press, which would be supplanted by a distraction story about fish dying in a polluted river."

"How much money did we give them?" asked Jay.

"Almost a billion and a half."

If it were Jess, she might have replied, "I don't get it. Why would we work against ourselves?" at which point Carter would have smiled at her naiveté. But it wasn't Jess. It was Ken, who lacked deep political savvy and occasionally appreciated learning more about how the world turned. He said, "Makes complete sense to me in the world of making money at the expense of your own nation."

Carter continued, "Paying off terrorists to stop being terrorists is not like paying farmers not to grow certain crops. We know there were a number of the highest level American politicians and businesspersons—all millionaires and billionaires—who wanted, even went out of their way, to ensure success of the terrorist. That's why we gave Iran the money in the first place. It's not complicated. I think these weapons are a small part of that."

Wei's computer-like mind processed his words. She came back with, "There's another part of this, too. You know better than us, but there are different categories of what are called weapons, both hard and soft. That long list of REEs on the manifest stands for Rare Earth Elements. REEs are a lot more abundant than gold, but harder than hell to mine in a decent concentration. Back then, they were used for magnets in computers, cars and turbines, lens making, and were also needed for computer chips.

"Many REEs are highly magnetic, others have special electrical-conductivity properties. There are 17 REEs on that list. Whoever has that load will make a great leap forward in technology, which means more accurate missiles, better spy satellites, computers, communications and so forth, while everybody else scrambles trying to scrape out a few REE for themselves.

"China refined maybe 80% of the world's REE. And Afghanistan had well over a trillion dollars-worth of them, all unmined. Cobalt is not an element that is part of that group, but it's listed here. Why? Because, he who controlled the world's cobalt controlled the batteries that operated the world's cell phones."

Trying to digest the magnitude of what Wei had told him, he couldn't come up with an intelligent reply, so Ken said, "Let's see if we can get in this place."

10

Constructed of reinforced concrete, the structure bragged three loading bays, the one on the north deeper than the other two on the east and west. Leaving the trucks behind and completing the circuit, Carter pulled in front of a large steel door on the south side and said, "I see at least two heavy locks. Why don't you see if those keys work before we go to Plan B?"

Ken tried one set of keys, shook his head and tried the second set to find the locks clicked open. Removing the padlocks, Ken swung open the heavy door only to find a second steel door with two more locks three feet behind the first. He tried the alternate set of keys to find success. He swung this door open, expecting to possibly find a third door. Instead, he looked into total blackness. The heady smell of foodstuffs hit them like a wall. Riki whined.

"Good job opening the doors, Ken," Jay quipped. Picking up on the droll sense of humor the two men frequently used, he added, "Civilized. And I always thought all you guys did was to pull out a crowbar from somewhere or kick down doors to get them open. I'll get a couple of lanterns."

The group moved slowly inside the vastness of the building, breathing shallowly, trying to move as swiftly as possible, while holding the lanterns up high, feeling like a team of archaeologists making their first entrance into an ancient tomb thousands of years old. Not necessarily unpleasant, the odor consisted of pine resin, possibly originating from wooden pallets, plus coffee, and a general mustiness composed of a myriad of undefined contributors.

Within a short time, their sense of smell became deadened as a defensive mechanism. Thousands of small and large sacks and cans were stacked in their respective places, virtually all labeled USDA, probably destined for the rail yard less than a half mile to the north. For several minutes, no one said a word, thunderstruck at the riches. Walking down the center aisle, the lantern light revealed banks of neons on the ceiling adorning the vastness of the immense cave.

Holding his own lantern, Ken moved off to the right and not long afterward, called out, "Hey, over here."

The others followed the light to find Ken. He pointed. Before them stood a double-wide padded freight elevator with doors open, easily large enough to contain a loaded forklift. "An elevator in a single story building?" Jay queried.

The men entered the elevator and checked the five buttons which read: G, B1, B2, B3, and B4.

"What was this place, a national repository?" Ken wondered, shaking his head. He seemed to be doing a lot of that lately. They all did. He thought for a moment and added, "With this size facility, there's got to be a couple of staircases."

"I wonder how that guy had the keys?" Jay asked.

"He may have worked here at the end," Wei said. She thought she had seen it all when she and Beth had worked the satellite downloads from Luke Air Force Base in the old days when the pair had a ringside seat to watch the end of the world. Now, a new revelation floored her. Carter immediately thought that if Jess were here to see this, she would began to cry at the enormity of it all.

"We are the keepers of the king's treasure," Carter mumbled.

"Why do you think the cavers were bringing the stuff to the restaurant?" asked Ken.

Jay replied, with a note of sarcasm in his voice, "Maybe the guys here wanted to offer it to us in trade for us letting them live in our little city."

Nobody responded for a moment, each in his or her own thoughts, until Carter said, "Yeah? Well maybe the caver guy, John, who tried to kill my wife and tell her they were going to take over our city, stepped on his dick and screwed the pooch for every one of his people."

"Wait, look at this," Wei announced, pointing to a wall by the elevator, where a laminated list hung on a clipboard. The list clearly identified and graphically depicted the numerous sectors, each defined by vertical and horizontal paths traversed by forklifts. Also listed were the contents of each sector. The map held one surprise of immense consequence—a cache of seeds, all of edible fruits, vegetables, and nut-bearing plants, possibly earmarked for under-developed countries, which, at this point, included their own. The map also identified the location of a second elevator, two loading bay doors, and the stairwells to the south of each elevator. It depicted the southernmost area where forklifts stood ready to move products.

Jay read out loud from the alphabetical list: "Amaranth, barley, buckwheat, bulgur, corn, couscous, millet, oats, quinoa, rice (brown and white), rye, soy, spelt, grain wheat, and wheat flour."

Wei gasped, putting a hand to her mouth. "That's all here?" she asked, rhetorically, turning around to look into the dark warehouse.

"Apparently so," Ken said. "Each in its own separate section. And it's all ours."

Jay stood staring at the words posted in front of him, speechless.

"This should keep our chefs busy. We're going to need more cooking pots," quipped Ken, trying to break through the superficial crust bordering an astounding event, trying to get his hands on the inner meat, perhaps to be found on the other floors.

"I'm guessing we're probably looking at 50,000 square feet of food, stacked to the ceiling in some quadrants," Jay calculated.

"This must have been a busy place in its day," Ken said. "No fast food here. Hmmm, it looks like there are offices on the north end. Let's check them out."

Three glass-enclosed offices with file cabinets were fully equipped with restrooms, desks, and rolling chairs. Occasional pictures on the wall taken from altitude, consisted of the railyard several miles to the west in downtown Flagstaff and of this building with scores of cars in the parking lot. Obviously the photographs were taken many years before. Ken took a moment to look at the photos in more detail to ensure there were no recent pictures of their own encampment. He began pulling open desk drawers when he heard Carter remark, "Jess should be here. The last time we did this she found a .45 and a nice bottle of Jack."

Ken had no problem remembering that Jess had almost killed, or at least shot, one of them, when she pulled a gun from the drawer and it went off. Finishing his inspection of the desk, he declared "Nothing here. Let's go." The sound of his voice failed to echo in the room filled with pallet-loads of products stacked two and three high, even more in some locations, challenging the ceiling.

The group descended a flight of 10 stairs to a landing followed by another 10 stairs to reach the door to Level B1. The odors on this floor consisted of a heavier smell of wood from the crates and pallets in their various sectors. Another posted and detailed sign noted that more than half the floor was devoted to hardware, but also graphically showed the presence of a cafeteria and restrooms, with forklifts parked to the south, similar to the floor above.

Ken pointed to one item on the list which read SPOTLIGHTS AND TRIPODS. "We may need those at some point," he remarked. The hardware included small and large generators, chain saws, thousands of feet of cable of varying sizes, bare and insulated wire, axes, hatchets, hammers, pliers, vice grips, ratchets and sockets, measured both in metric and SAE, socket wrenches, compression gauges, humidity meters, drills, nuts, bolts, torque wrenches, and screws of every ilk, bags of concrete and mortar, and, sans lumber, virtually all items one would need to build a house or repair a car.

"This one has its own loading bay, according to the map. Let's check out the cafeteria area." Carter led the others to the north end of the large room. Surveying its size, he stated the obvious. "There're enough tables and chairs here to feed half our population."

He had his hand on door handle of one of the large freezers, about to open it, when Jay said, "I wouldn't open the door."

Carter removed his hand as though the metal were hot. "Right. I don't think we'd like smelling what's inside." He had a vision of an archaeologist who opened the doors of a tomb housing mummies wrapped in cloth contaminated with countless mold spores, only to die of infection later. *The curse of the mummies.*

Another surprise came on Level B2 when a pungent odor hit them. Instantly their eyes teared and caused them to cough. "Let's make this fast," Wei remarked.

"What stinks?" Ken asked.

Wei replied, "It's formaldehyde. It makes sense because we've got a floor full of clothing. Formaldehyde was once used for the making of hundreds of products for color enhancement, as a fire-retardant, and for the making of permanent press materials. I don't care if the stuff is crated or not, it'll leach through."

"We'd need full-face gas masks, if we ever came back here again," Ken declared, coughing.

"No problem," Wei contributed. "Tell me how many you think you'll need and I'll pick up some good painter's masks from different Home Depots and other supply stores and reseed them with fresh activated charcoal. For eye protection, we can use swimming goggles."

Jay shrugged. That's why she's the brains of the outfit."

The lists noted that boxed and crated clothing, received directly from the manufacturer, was ready for shipment to parts unknown, including blue jeans, both tan and camouflage cargo pants and work shirts, Tee-shirts, boots and work socks, sneakers and belts, all of different sizes. All the clothing appeared to be meant for the serious worker, not somebody interested in fashion design or Hawaiian prints.

Staring at the list, Carter said, "My wife has been complaining to me about wanting a new wardrobe."

Jay remarked, "Same here," only to receive a poke in the ribs from Wei.

Wei remarked, "When we get back, I'll get a couple of the girls to start taking measurements. We can plan a return trip and supply our extended family with new clothes."

"It won't be easy collecting individual items," Ken said. "We'll have to open a lot of crates."

"What else you got to do?" Carter stated.

Carter suggested, "The next trip here will have to include a large number of people, because I want a written copy of everything on the lists of contents on each floor. It would be nice if we had a camera, but we don't, so it will have to be done with one person reading and one person writing. Put a team on each floor to expedite it."

"Why waste the manpower," Jay said, off-handedly. "Wei and I will remember the lists and copy them into notebooks when we get home."

"Damn siders make me sick," Carter muttered, jokingly, loud enough for them to hear.

Happy to leave the pungent odors of B2, the entourage entered the stale, but un-fouled air of the stairwell to descend to Level B3.

Mixed with the scent of wooden crates on pallets stacked two high nearing the eight foot ceiling at times, the unmistakable odor of machine oil greeted them. Not as pungent as the vapors of formaldehyde encountered on the previous floor, the heaviness of the stale air, unrefreshed by any outdoor air exchange for many years, still made it difficult to breathe deeply.

"Anybody's guess," Jay remarked.

"Auto parts," Wei threw out.

The four entered the massive third basement cavern hoping to find another list posted next to the elevator.

"It's like the coded list you showed us upstairs, isn't it, Ken?" Jay asked. "It's a bunch of numbers and letters."

"You could start or end a small war with what's in this room. It's a wonder this place never exploded, "Wei exclaimed.

"It would leave a hell of a crater if it did," Ken commented.

Carter understood the more intricate nature of government operations than did Ken. He explained, "This floor is definitely a separate operation. That's why everything is heavily coded and secreted. I'll guarantee somebody did their best to keep the workers from knowing what was here. Either an independent company or highly paid government black-ops personnel were hired to run this place. This floor is the cash cow of the operation. The rest is a cover, probably set up by somebody close to the top of the food chain."

"What a species," Wei remarked, having shared the watching of its demise with Beth years before on the satellite downloads from Luke Air Force Base. She began to walk the isles. "Where are you going?"

Jay called after her.

"I have to see the electronics section; see how hard it is to get a cetain crate," she called back over her shoulder.

Jay shrugged and followed after her, passing sectors of neatly stacked large and small wooden cases, long and short crates, and drums of various sizes, until she stopped at one and closely inspected the numbers and letters printed on the wood. Patting the box, she said, "This is the one I want. It's full of play toys," and continued walking along the east-west aisle to reach one running along the north wall.

Jay turned to see Carter and Ken several yards behind them. "Here's another steel door. I didn't see this on the map," he called, finding the door locked.

Carter grinned, "Let's try the other single key, Ken."

11

The key fit and the four found themselves in a long concrete corridor four feet wide with a narrow-gage rail track running down the middle, similar to one might see in a coal mine. Several yards down each side a door could be found on opposite sides of the track to total four rooms in all.

Using the same key, Ken unlocked the first door on the left and held the lantern high. An inoperable light switch was set in the wall to his left. The existing light revealed stacks of cocaine bricks similar to those he and Jess had discovered in the loft of the barn. Here were many times that number. The other rooms contained more cocaine, jars and packages of opioids, methamphetamines, black tar heroin, LSD, hashish, fentanyl, opium, and a variety of popular drugs, each clearly labeled as such. No mistaking one for another.

"Why would anyone ship this stuff out to a whistle stop, because, I'll bet if we follow this tunnel northward, it will lead to the tracks," Wei said.

Jay added, "Right. I would think it would have been a lot easier to buy it directly from the bad guys rather than having to go through this place, unless this is an intermediate point; however, I will admit the movement of illicit drugs isn't my area of expertise."

"I'll answer that," Carter announced. "It wasn't a whistle stop outlet. It was major port of entry because this shit wasn't getting sent out like the rest of the stuff in this warehouse, *it was coming in.* I say this operation pulled in tens of millions of dollars in term of drug distribution, never mind the weapons. From here, it got trucked out to anywhere. I'll bet a high percentage of all the big rigs that ran the highways back then were carrying some type of contraband."

Jay asked, "How is this connected to the rest of everything else here?"

"We could make a case either way," Carter shrugged. Then he added, "Come on. One more flight," and headed for the door to the stairwell.

Level B4 proved to be the mechanical room, which contained enough sleeping machinery to operate the entire building, destined to remain that way for a long time.

With his pickup filled with passengers, Carter drove back to the truck stop to recover the half-track and the van, then the caravan headed for home, with the crate Wei wanted loaded in the back.

Within the hour, having been informed of their

arrival, a crowd formed around the three vehicles. The adventurers began to unload, hailed as heroes who brought new food stores from a different source, one uncontaminated by a terrible toxin. Willing volunteers unloaded sacks of flour, rice, kidney beans, corn, millet, and rye; a 40-pound cloth bag labeled Brazilian Coffee Beans, large cans of hot chocolate, kilos of pinto beans, and containers of sugar. Every sack and container was stamped USDA.

Not the least excited were the chefs who could prepare kiln-baked breads and pastries for a grand fiesta with plenty remaining to last a long time. It appeared the would-be marauders might have been planning to move. But to where? Sekah City, perhaps?

Their new stores had survived for many years, now requiring the same care that a new home had been found for them at the compound. If exposed to too much moisture, the foodstuffs and their containing bags would rapidly become fodder for ants and other insects, mice, rats, bacteria, mold, and a variety of other life forms. After some discussion, a work crew moved the sacks and condiments to a single room in the residence hall along with a space heater dedicated to reducing moisture, and placed the room under lock and key.

Time tugged on the strings, playing them like marionettes, demanding attention be paid to the issue of survival. Once the foodstuffs were secure, the following day, Carter, Ken, and Gregor, along with Carla and Riki, returned to the warehouse, this time to walk the length of the half-mile tunnel northward. The roads leading to the point where the tunnel might lead were likely impassable requiring the usage of lanterns to make their way through the arrow-straight passageway. Avoiding the rails, the men found it easy going, albeit sweating in the stifling air, the ceiling height barely clearing their heads, all 6'2" or taller.

Twenty minutes later they arrived at a fifth steel door. Like the others, a wall switch had once been used to turn on numerous recessed lights which once illuminated a roomful of weapons for immediate use and not for shipment. These included a variety of handguns of various calibers, rifles, sub-machine guns and sniper rifles with scopes. Loaded magazines sat next to each of the weapons. Ken and Carter checked the action on a number of them and found them to still operate smoothly, an indication of recent usage, while the lubricant on others had oxidized making the action harder to operate. Gregor fumbled with several, not familiar with the weapons. He received patient instructions from his friends, not missing an opportunity to school a man of Gregor's talent.

"Why are the bullets in the magazines different than the others?" queried Gregor.

Ken slid out one of the rounds from a magazine to hold it in front of him. "These have a hollow tip which enables them to fragment when a target is struck. This causes greater damage and dictates that the round will not pass through, but will dissipate all its energy into the target. It also means that somebody has finished practicing and is ready for action, which raises a red flag, because somebody might have another key to this place."

Carter added "Or somebody is getting ready to defend this warehouse."

"Or, you already got the guys at the truck stop who were doing the practicing," suggested Gregor, an idea that felt a lot more comfortable to believe than the other ideas.

To the rear of the room stood still another door leading to a small shooting range measuring 20' by 50'. Entering the room, they saw the wall hanging. As one, the three moved slowly toward it, holding the lanterns at various heights. Somebody had cut a three-foot square of paper from a roll. Onto the paper, an architect or an artist, or both, presented a to-scale detailed layout of their compound, Sekah City, replete with buildings, trailers, both greenhouses, turkey farm, cars, river, bridge, water wheels, windmills, front end loader, gun safes, the Big House and barn, everything. Arrows flowed from several directions into the compound. None flowed outward. Ken removed the picture and rolled it up to post later in the meeting hall, possibly with a frame. In the weapons room, he found a length of string to tie it off. "That was thoughtful of these kind folks to think of us," he said. "I hope to return the favor someday."

"I think we already started," Gregor said, after an instant of contemplation. "After all, one of them did loan you his keys."

Carter said, "This entire enterprise was construct-ed a good half-century ago. You know there had to be dark money involved, possibly with international contributions. I wonder how many more buildings are out there like this."

Before the others could answer, Gregor said, "I smelled gunpowder in there. Why would any-one want to practice shooting in a place with poor lighting, especially when you have a whole world to shoot at."

"I can think of several reasons," Ken replied. "Whoever built this or uses it, might not want any-body to hear you or see you, and you might be old-school. You grew up shooting at bullseyes and cutouts of humans, and by god, you're going keep shooting at the same kinds of targets until the real deal comes along."

Exiting the weapons room, Ken closed and re-locked the door. Not completely satisfied with the explanation he had given, he set the rolled-up map on the floor for later pickup. Only a dozen paces away, a hatch was set into the ceiling at the tunnel's end. A flat car stood on the tracks several feet back from it. Ken tried to push up the hatch. Finding it re-sistant, he pushed harder and got his shoulder into it, finally clearing enough space to see a rug had cov-ered it. He cleared the area, looked around, and then pushed it up all the way. Sunlight flooded in, tempo-rarily blinding the men. He told the dogs to leap up through the hatch opening onto the ground, which both did easily. Carter and Gregor extinguished the lanterns and left them behind.

The small group found themselves in an office. A stone's throw before them stood a majestic diesel-powered locomotive trailing a single boxcar. Standing 16 feet in height and weighing well over 200 tons, the red behemoth was breathtaking in its majesty, although it's presence came as a slight surprise.

"Is that for real?" Gregor exclaimed. "I mean, I've seen pictures before but this is crazy."

Carter found the simple response amusing. At the same time, he wondered how he would survive if he had to live below ground for years. Probably not very well. "Countless trains a day came through here back in the day. I mean, right through the center of town."

Ken explained, "No doubt that train hauled the goods our friends brought up from the tunnel. Back in the day, one or more locomotives could be hooked onto well over 100 cars, all fully loaded, going across the country every day."

He stopped his explanation when Gregor asked, "Why only one car on that one?"

Ken didn't answer. Instead, he cautiously moved closer to the entrance of the open air office, the glass long-since shattered. "Let's check it out," he said.

"I'll go," Carter answered. "Carla, Riki, stay here."

Carter opened the door, took a moment to look both ways, and quickly walked 30 yards to the locomotive. He climbed up into the enclosed cab and spent a number of minutes examining the controls. At last, he looked out the windows on all sides and not seeing anyone, looked back at Gregor and Ken who both gave the thumbs up sign.

He quickly opened the door, climbed down to the ground and strode back to inspect the boxcar. Sliding open the door he saw sacks of grains and various condiments along with two kilos of cocaine wrapped in plastic. He noted a great deal of blood at the edge of the doorway to the left where a small, sharp piece of metal stuck out from the door track that may have come off of something they shipped, and now rode along with the door. This would explain the cut to Kody's arm.

Returning to the office, he reported what he found and offered, "I'm thinking a whole bunch of things. First, somebody here is an engineer and knows how to start and run this thing."

Ken said, "The way I read it, your buddy ripped his arm open so they had to pull back to the restaurant where we caught up with them. The injury must have interrupted their workday. There's still another day left for them to make their delivery, but to where?"

"We find cocaine everywhere we look," complained Gregor. "In the trunks up in the loft, in the tunnel room, and here. And poor Danny. Why is there no much?"

Carter said, severely, "Because, my friend, this used to be a major drug-trafficking corridor along with what used to be Seattle, Los Angeles, Houston, New Orleans, Miami, New York, Yuma . . . hell man, hundreds of tons a day got shipped in, easy. And that was only coke."

"Something else, too," said Ken. "There are too many goodies to serve a few guys living it up somewhere. This train made one stop to serve a lot of people. I'm not saying they took the train every time, but two kilos of coke can serve a lot of people for a long time."

Gregor said, "The train's heading east. Why don't we see what's out there?"

"If these guys found the bodies in the restaurant, we could be in trouble," Ken said.

"No argument there," Carter admitted, then added, "The engine is actually running. The only thing I know about these 16-cylinder diesels is that they're left on, unless parked for some time. But for regular usage, it's kept idling so we don't need to mess with trying to start a cold engine. Obviously, we interrupted their return trip."

Ken said, "Let's see if we can find out where they were going."

12

Carter announced, "I'll call Jess and tell her we might be late for dinner. We'll make a little exploratory run, but try to stay out of a fight. Gregor, pull out the map and let's look at what's ahead. Also, let's see if we can find an operation manual for a locomotive here somewhere."

Twenty minutes later Ken read from the book and the train began to move. Although the men climbed into the cab, the dogs easily made the jump up without assistance. Gregor stood watch with the restless dogs, unable to see anything from their low perspective. Keeping the throttle between 15 and 20 miles per hour, Carter drove the train smoothly into a darkening sky. To him the moment appeared surreal. Here he was, driving a train, no less, in a cabin not designed to hold three men and two dogs. The setting sun behind him had expanded to twice its size, magnified and reddened by the windblown ash in the air still present after the forest fire. The altered sunlight reflected off the gray ash and white cloud layer covering the eastern portion of the sky ahead of them turning the underside of the clouds red-orange and the entire world red. The sound of the train on the tracks and the swaying motion mesmerized him, until Ken brought him out of his reverie.

"We stole a train," Ken said.

"True, but only a small one," Carter quipped, flashing back to reality. "Probably a misdemeanor, not a felony."

Ken remarked, "A storm's moving in fast and we're coming up to the big marketplace shown on the map. Look at that four-lane road, it's totally pot-holed. No wonder they took the train rather than a vehicle. Even a half-track would have a rough time going over it. "

Carter said, "Why don't you read the book and tell me how to stop this thing fast if I have to. And while you're at it, tell me how to put it in reverse."

Short minutes later, Carter stopped the train a quarter-mile from the big marketplace and said, "I'm guessing maybe 50 or 60 stores in there. Usual mall types. Probably less if the roof caved from snow weight like the rest of them did."

"Gregor, hand me those binos," Ken requested.

Gregor slung off his backpack and reached in to pull out the binoculars, which he handed to Ken. A moment later Ken said, "There are two guys leaning against the hood of a military troop carrier on the far side facing away from us smoking and drinking out of bottles." He handed the binoculars to Carter, who looked for a moment, and passed them to Gregor.

Ken said, "Let's send in the dogs."

Carter agreed. "Good call. We want to be out of sight when it happens, so once we let them go, we'll back up slowly. The dogs will catch up to us soon enough."

"Wait," Gregor said. "Another man came out of the entrance with a bottle in his hand. He's talking with the two men."

Carter knelt down and spoke to both Carla and Riki, giving them basic instructions. Wagging their tales in understanding, Ken opened one of the doors and the dogs jumped from the locomotive onto the gravel and ran toward the distant truck. Carter immediately put the train in reverse and began to back up slowly while Ken followed the progress of the dogs sent on a mission to kill, like thermal imaging cameras located on missiles homing in on their targets.

The dogs split up, bounding over jutting pieces of asphalt and dodging holes, one heading to the front of the truck and one to the rear, both emerging at the same time to attack. All Ken could see for the next few seconds was humans scrambling, dogs either flying through the air or disappearing from sight with not a single shot heard. Within three minutes of their departure the dogs came running back to the train, over the broken roadway, leaping and skirting around potholes, racing toward the train.

Finally, Carter stopped to allow the dogs to leap onboard to get congratulatory hugs while Ken kept watching. "Several more men came out. . . .must have heard screams."

"I'll bet whoever is left in there is freaking paranoid about coming outside anymore," Gregor said, having acquired Topsider lingo and in awe at what had just happened, "Can you imagine seeing three of your friends ripped to pieces without any evidence of seeing who or what did it, afraid to ever come out again. If any survived, all they could say is that two wild wolves came out of nowhere and attacked them."

Ken suggested, "Whoever is left probably has enough supplies to last a considerable amount of time, so disabling the truck wouldn't starve them out, but it would keep them locked in place and might discourage these guys from doing us any harm. It sure beats going into their home and not having any idea what to expect?"

Carter said, "It looks like a hard rain is coming. Let's sit here for a little while, maybe go outside with the dogs and stay close. Once it starts, we'll move in again. Ken, see if you can find anything in the book about *not* turning on the headlight of this beast."

"How about if I go in and pull the rotor from the distributor on the truck. I'll take the dogs with me," offered Gregor, enthusiastically.

Ken chuckled, "Beats letting the air out of their tires. They might try to start the truck, but it'll take them forever to figure out what's wrong. Let them hike out and brave the elements knowing wild wolves will eat them, or stay there until hell freezes over. You'll have to make your way over the rubble, so be careful. Then, you get the honors of backing up the train."

"Really?" Gregor exclaimed, flabbergasted. "I didn't have a chance to practice driving trains much where I grew up," he remarked, with a grin.

"We could always go back and pick up some of those heavier weapons. I really want to finish these guys off," Carter offered.

Ken said, snidely, "Yeah, we can also lock 'em in and burn down the building. But we're not going to. Tell you what, though. If you see any of them again you can have your way. By the way, you insisted that you and Jess could deal with Brenda alone. What did happen to her?"

"Nothing good," Carter summarized, with a twist to his mouth, a habit he displayed as a tell whenever he had crossed a line.

Ken and Gregor exchanged knowing glances. Their lips were sealed.

"Let me see that map again." Carter took the map from Ken and held it up to the remaining light coming through the engine's windows. "Here's a possible problem. The rail lines not only serve Sedona, but also serve Verde Valley."

"Which means what?" Gregor asked.

Ken replied, "Which means these assholes know about where we live and how many of us there are and have a detailed picture of our home, and doubtless know our activities and there may be another nest in a place where we are thinking about moving to."

Both men concurred.

At least one more contingent of bad guys required elimination. If good people can cluster to form a community, so can bad people. However, should the occasion arise where one of the enemy could be saved, well, that's a bridge to be crossed at a later time.

Carter inserted, "It also means the three of us are going to take a drive down there soon. We're going to bring Wei and Jay along to operate the drones. I have an idea that may keep us from getting into a shootout, but we'll have to move fast. If somebody doesn't get a shipment, they may get curious and start looking our way ahead of schedule. Ken, hand me the sat phone."

13

Jess's head was splitting. She'd spent long hours in the medical office reading about human diseases and wasn't in the mood to spend hours making up her witches' brew for an upcoming mission. At least Carter could have given her a couple of days warning, not "We need it now, Hon, We'll be back as soon as we can to help."

She caught herself getting sucked into the void and took a deep breath to calm herself. This time it didn't work. She felt great anger, even rage—a dark emotion she had never encountered prior to coming to the surface—directing her attention toward those who might bring terror to *her people.*

Like the first time, once engaged in her work, she couldn't be certain of the dosage she had prepared from the numerous species of mushrooms in her possession, she only hoped it would be sufficient to cause more than headaches. Sometimes, the most serious effects, like liver and kidney failure, didn't occur until long after the event. Would they have to wait days, even weeks? She could read between the lines. If this failed, the war might be short. On the other hand, eight intelligent pre-programmed sider dogs could do a hell of lot of damage when turned loose. That thought gave her cause to smile, noticing her headache had disappeared.

The application of her new preparation differed from the first. If Danny were alive, he might say there is a big difference in terms of time and symptoms between an agent consumed by the digestive route versus one consumed by the respiratory route.

The drive home had become difficult and slow going. The downpour, coupled with lightning flashes and cracking thunder, made it all the more difficult to console the dogs. When they did arrive at the meeting hall to drop off Gregor, the dogs fairly flew out of the car in their effort to escape. He didn't need the animals getting wet and shaking-off inside the house to run around while delicate work needed to be accomplished.

He next parked in front of the house, rather than in his usual spot in the parking area outside the circle of boulders. When he and Ken did enter, Jay had already spread a sheet of plastic on the living room floor with a bag of coke resting on it. After a few minutes of getting their bearings and reporting their discoveries along with the dogs' activities, the team set to work.

Carter opened the package and slowly poured

the contents onto the sheet, trying to prevent the white dust from becoming airborne. The more Jess worked, the better she felt. She had a chemist's idea of how to add her two concoctions to the powder. She had chosen several species of *Amanita* and other toxic mushrooms available in the forest, each with differing chemicals from hallucinogens to flat out nasty poisons.

With the use of an eye dropper, she deliberately added the liquid of her first concoction to various areas of the spread-out powder. Jay and Carter continually moved the powder around, ensuring its complete mixture and to avoid the formation of clumps by going over it with a rolling pin. During the process, she also tapped out small portions of finely ground mushrooms consisting of the stem and the cap, her second concoction. First she had minced the mushrooms into small pieces she further cut with a razor blade. Because 90 % of a mushroom's weight is water, she needed to dry a number of them under low heat to be followed by a grinding in her own mortar and pestle. She obtained a fine off-white dust, definitely unnoticeable when mixed with the large mass of cocaine.

Two hours later, Jess had exhausted her supplies. The men repackaged the powder and re-taped it to make it appear as though it had come directly from Colombia. Carter handed the finished product to Ken and the group slept until breakfast. By then, the storm had broken and only a strong northerly wind remained.

Using the map as a guide, Carter, Jay and Wei took the 30 minute drive to Cottonwood. Ken and Gregor followed in the van, which contained sacks of produce and boxes of condiments from their own stores. The shipment also included a single deadly bag of seeded cocaine along with stacks of hundred dollar bills, all to entice their subjects to have disagreements. Everyone prepared for a long stay.

Most of the residential sectors lay in jumbled heaps, but a number of retail stores still stood, either in their entirety, or partially. The latter included the Home Depot shopping complex several members of their group had visited a number of times. Using it as a base of operations, both vehicles parked in the lot. Wei launched the big drone used earlier in Flagstaff and Jay launched the smaller one used for surveillance of the Big House, trying to look for moving vehicles, or those out of place in a particular setting, such as large trucks or military vehicles.

The drones flew north and east, but no suspicious activity or out-of-place trucks appeared on either monitor. Returning to home base for recharging, the drones were next sent west and south.

Another pass or two by the drones could eliminate the small city from consideration—with the exception of residential outlying areas where no retail stores stood—at which point surveillance would have to be moved southeast to Camp Verde.

Suddenly, two military troop carriers appeared parked one behind the other on one side of a restaurant attached to the Best Western Hotel, only a short distance from their present location. A small swimming pool, drained of water, stood between the front office/restaurant complex and two buildings to the rear where two floors of rooms were available. To those observing the monitors, it would appear their antagonists preferred the open space of a restaurant combined with the kitchen facility as opposed to the comfort of two men to a single guest room; probably because management could maintain a more watchful eye on their comrades who were likely mercenaries recruited from hell itself. What they were doing or planning could be anybody's guess. There was nothing left to conquer or steal. The only known other group of humans in the area were those in Sekah City, a city complete unto itself, and those in the mall already visited. Might there be a third?

Ken offered, "Looks like basic two-and-a-half-ton carriers, good for maybe 14 men in back and a couple or so in the front. Maybe 30 men total."

"Let's prepare for the worst," Carter replied.

"As always," Ken returned.

One drone flew while another recharged until early evening. An argument among two of the men occurred at one point directly in front of the intact windows of the structure, to result in the knifing of one of them, who dropped to the ground, but who apparently still lived. Images showed him continuing to move. The surviving man walked inside the restaurant to return with two more who carried the body to a nearby ditch, spoke for a few minutes, and then returned to their domicile.

After dark, the van and dually stopped to within 200 yards of the restaurant with the lights off. Leaving the engines idling, the five went to work. Gently closing the car doors to extinguish the interior lights, the group was fortunate. The normally strong breeze had increased in intensity to help cover their approach an hour after the last light had gone out in the restaurant. Over a single trip, small sacks of grain and a box of condiments were deposited outside the restaurant, along with the bag of coke. Then, out of sight on the side of the building, Gregor collected two more rotors from the trucks' distributors to add to his collection. An old hand experienced in this matter by this point, he accomplished the thefts by moonlight.

The group stealthily returned to their respective transports and without the sound of an engine starting or door closing, the vehicles slowly drove off into the night heading for home. Tomorrow could prove to be interesting.

The direct inhalation of psilocybin combined with cocaine has completely different effects on the brain and body than does the ingestion of mushroom toxins alone. There is a synergistic effect when the drugs instantly pass the blood-brain barrier. Within seconds extreme paranoia occurs along with the release of pent up hostilities, combined with euphoria and a thrill of killing, even self-mutilation. The nervous system becomes confused, even randomized in its behavior. Brain functions violate their traverses along normal neural pathways. Logical thought disappears, similar to the effect of alcohol negating the decision-making process of the brain that tells a person to stop drinking. Extreme psychedelic visions become common in some. In others, hostile behaviors come to the fore in those whose minds are steeped with such experiences. Raging tempests demand to be satisfied and the habitual nature of the drug demands more and more be inhaled until death do us part.

14

The well-armed war party of five returned in the morning. Their first task: survey the restaurant by drone from their parking lot base of operations. Several bodies lay outside. Others lay as far as a hundred yards down the street and yet another behind the wheel of one of the trucks, unable to escape. The front windows of the building were shattered, ostensibly by gunfire.

"What do you feel like doing, Carter, driving through the front door?" Ken asked.

"There's a safer way. Wei, why don't you keep the big drone in the sky for a look-over, and Jay, run the small one in there right through the open front window."

Moments later, watching the monitor, Gregor exclaimed under his breath, "My God, what a mess. I think I'm going to throw up."

"War is hell," Ken answered.

Gregor had previously asked Ken if there wasn't

an alternative to killing everyone to which Ken had replied, "I wish there were. We can't leave them alone because they're getting ready to overrun our city. If we captured them all, what would be do with them, even if they laid down their arms and promised to be good from now on? We can't pick and choose who should go to therapy sessions. We can't let them scatter because we'd be looking over our shoulder every minute of every day."

Gregor had no counter argument. Now he said, "What do we do with the place, burn it down?"

"It's not a bad idea, even if we have to burn down a perfectly good hotel nobody will ever use again. I can tell you right now, I'm not digging any graves, not for those guys," Ken snorted.

"What now? Now we go in," Carter said. "There may be one or two we can save. Gregor, first we collect the weapons to ensure we don't get shot, then we inspect the bodies for signs of life."

Gregor cautiously followed the other two into the restaurant. Several minutes later, the men piled an assortment of handguns, rifles, and knives outside. The knives included two Bowies, an Arkansas toothpick, three machetes, and an assortment of pocket knives. Ken directed, "Gregor, collect the weapons from those in the street, then bring the van. We'll load them into it and bring them here. Let's find the food we brought. It would seem nobody had an appetite."

Gregor did as requested while Ken and Carter examined the bodies for signs of life. A moment later,

Carter called on the radio, "Wei, keep up the surveillance. Jay, bring the medical kit. We have a live one here. It's a head wound."

When Carter bent over the man, he saw the eyes were open. When the man saw him, he reached down to his holster to find it empty. Carter said, "You're the only one alive. I can fix that problem if you want me to." At which point, the man relaxed.

Jay arrived with a medical kit and handed the man a bottle of water. When he saw Jay was a sider he shrank back, but still drank his fill. Jay dressed his wound and wrapped a bandage around his head, then he and Carter helped the man to his feet where he stood for several moments. Ken and Carter assisted the man outside while Jay went to the kitchen to see what he could find of use and soon had several boxes of new Sterno cans. He did find a large Swiss Army Knife in its own sheath, which he immediately attached to his belt.

Gregor arrived with the van, and Ken announced, "After we interview this guy, we'll collect the other bodies and bring them here. We're going to burn down the place."

Carter asked the man, "What's your name?"

"Jim Wright," he answered. He tended toward the stocky side with thick forearms, square cut jaw, blood-shot blue eyes, and a mop of black hair in disarray. If he cleaned up, the man might be good looking.

"Why don't you tell us what happened?" Carter asked. He needed information and had become weary of guessing. He also had the sudden urge to kill the man and be done with it.

"Who are you?" Jim asked, interrupting Carter's struggle to decide which way he should end this man's life.

"We're the people who may save your life, but the day is still young. Now talk," Ken replied, towering over Jim, not caring to disguise is true feelings in niceties.

Jim began, "We were here maybe a month, getting bored to death, waiting for a go sign to take over some place near Sedona. Our boss had this map and said those guys were always changing things over there so he needed to have another meeting with a faction as big as ours. Their leader said they want the place for themselves. Everybody wants to go in shooting. I guess they have guns at the encampment. I mean, there's supposed to be housing for a lot of people and they grow their own food."

"What's his name, your boss?" Ken asked.

"Kody Davis," Jim answered.

"He's dead and so are most of the people in the other 'faction' you call it," Gregor said.

"How'd they die, do you know?"

"Kody and a few of his buddies ate some bad food that didn't agree with them. Several of the guys in the other faction got eaten by dogs. We saw it happen," Carter said, stretching the truth somewhat.

Jim looked surprised, but refrained from asking too many questions of his own. He went on, "Kody made sure we got our supplies of food and coke, but last night we got a bad batch along with a bunch of money. The money sparked the argument when everybody tore into the blow. I don't do that coke shit. Hard liquor is fine with me. Anyway, about a few minutes after the other guys tore into it, everything fell apart. The stabbings and shootings lasted maybe a minute overall. I tried to defend myself, but I started drinking early and couldn't shoot straight. I think I was one of the last to get hit."

Ken asked, "Where did you come from and why aren't there any women?"

Jim answered, "We were hooked up with Kody since before the Great Catastrophe. He said he was a hero in the Rangers and a commanding officer. He took charge of everything. The guy was strange. He always had a diamond stud in one ear and a ruby stud in the other. We lived in this huge cave in the Verde Valley all these years, fishing, hunting, chopping wood, cooking, scavenging, trying not to kill each other. That last part didn't always work. A bunch of guys took off years ago and, from what I heard, found some other caves near the place where Kody wanted to attack, but his plans kept changing, in part because lot of those other guys got wiped out. As far as the other, he thought women were bad luck and never wanted any in the group. There weren't a lot of them running around, anyway."

Jim went on with his tale. "One of our guys, not Kody, was a hot shot at some big warehouse up in Flagstaff. He would bring us anything we wanted. He knew how to run a train, too, and would bring

us our stuff by rail until the last quake here recently took out the tracks at some point. So we had to
move all our gear to this hotel. I wanted to get away
from Kody and offered to move in with the other
group, but he told me to stay with them because I
could sew up people. You wouldn't know it by looking at me, but I used to be a physical therapist and
fitness coach. Anyway, one day our warehouse guy
disappeared and Kody showed up with the keys. He
scared us. The man would shoot you if you looked
at him sideways."

"How did you cope with the winters in the cave?"
Ken asked.

"No problem. Two of them were linked like some
giant vein of limestone ran through the mountain that
maybe got washed out by water a long time ago. The
hole became a U-shaped pair of caves connected at
the middle so the heat went mostly in one direction.
The side we were using held as many as 40 of us at
one time, no problem, until the number started to get
whittled down."

Carter couldn't contain himself and told Jim the
true story about Kody and the Rangers, to which
Jim replied, "Figures. A nut case like him would get
weeded out of any military organization. I never believed it, anyway, the way he bragged about himself.
Myself, I served in the regular army as a medic and
saw some action overseas. Don't ask me why I got
in with Kody. I guess he spun a good web and it
seemed like the thing to do at the time, I mean, to
hole up until everything got straight again. The trou-

ble is, it never did."

"When was the last time you practiced medicine, if practice is the right word?" asked Carter.

"Shit, are you kidding me? Around here, all the time, man," Jim answered. "That's why I got recruited."

"How many more of you are there? How many more nests do we have to worry about?" Ken inquired.

"Who are you guys, anyway? How did you come to rescue me?" Jim wanted to know.

"Answer the question," Carter ordered.

Gregor, who had arrived earlier and stood by the door postulated, "The guy knows too much. He's holding out. When I grew up underground," here he paused in sad remembrance of a city that had raised him, "I was the biggest kid in town. I won all my wrestling and boxing matches, but, in truth, I didn't like to fight. I only wanted to write songs and draw sketches. In order to avoid fights, I learned a little psychology. I learned how to read people from their eye movements to their body gestures to the tones of their voices, maybe read their intent, despite their words alone. This man is holding back. He is reticent about giving certain information. He may be using it as a bargaining chip.

"If it was up to me, I wouldn't give him too much too soon. The guy spent years among thieves and murderers, men who made up stories about themselves and others. I don't think he'll flip into a righteous human overnight. Maybe he needs to see

Kody's body before he's convinced. He may think you're lying about his death and a lot more, and if so, Kody may come after him. He's steeped in suspicion."

Jim responded by orating, "I know we were getting ready to make a move on this place he was scoping out and he warned us about a couple of hotshot military dudes there and some others who know how to shoot straight. There's also some nasty bitch who shot one of our guys after a couple of sider dogs ate him and then chewed others to pieces before some of them got away. There are even a couple of sider people in that place, if you can believe that. He told us there was one particular guy over there he wanted for himself. Say, wait a minute. You guys aren't . . . "

All men stared at their captive and only grinned.

Jim's dark eyes widened in surprise and his thin lips parted to show good teeth. Smiling, Carter said, "I'm the guy he wanted saved and served up and that nasty bitch is my wife. If you behave yourself, you may get to work with her practicing medicine. If you don't, she and the dogs will be practicing on you," at which point Jim's eyes rolled upward and he passed out. Gregor caught him before his head hit the concrete.

Jim awakened after Ken threw water on his face. Once he got his bearings, Jim thankfully received a bottle of water from Gregor, who said, "He never answered the last question. How many more do you know about that are not here, or in the Flagstaff area?"

To Ken and Carter, Gregor had elevated himself, almost overnight, from a songwriter and artist, to a hardened person with a military-like mind.

Carter looked at Jim, then downward, shaking his head, in a classic pose of a person who had reached the limits of his ability to cope with life. Exhaling, and pulling out a knife in a sheath at his belt, he said, "Jim, my friend, in about five seconds, I'm going to ask my two associates to leave. I seriously want you and me to get to know each other. Unfortunately, you will not be pleased with the relationship. By the way, I also want to know the answer to the question."

Jim looked from one to the other back to Carter. He saw only cold impenetrable steel in their eyes and the set of their jaws. *Crunch time. Reality had spoken.*

"Okay, okay." Jim confessed, "There's another group of us. Maybe a dozen, maybe fifteeen, I'm not sure. They're laying low, scoping your home ground for attack, waiting for the word to be given."

"Who gives the word? " Ken asked.

"If Kody's dead, it has to be one of their own bunch. They didn't care about him, anyway, that's why they split off when Kody moved us down here," Jim said.

"When do they plan to attack?" Ken asked.

"It could be anytime," Jim confessed.

"Where are they holed up?" Carter demanded.

"I swear I don't know. Could be here in town, could be anywhere?" Jim admitted.

Carter nodded. "One thing they don't know about is our secret weapons." He pulled out his sat phone and walked off to the side to let Jess know of the developments.

When Carter returned, Ken remarked, "We're going to have to take him back with us. Where do we put him?"

15

An hour later the bodies were collected from the street and joined their dead comrades in the restaurant, the guns were emptied of ammo and joined their owners in the building while the food stores were piled into the van. The troop carriers were moved to the next street to be collected on another date and the restaurant, doused in fuel oil, was set ablaze.

Ken quipped, "After this we'll have enough vehicles to start a car dealership."

Carter advised, "True, although business could be in a dull for a few years, so don't quit your day job."

Less than a minute later, Jim got in between Jay and Wei, cringing as he did so, and Carter followed his directions to the cave with Ken and Gregor following. Along the way, Carter pulled out the sat phone and said, "Hi, Hon, we're all okay. Got business taken care of thanks to you. We'll be bringing home a guest. A survivor." He turned in the seat to look back at Jim, winked, and said, "It's my bitch wife. I'm sure she wants to meet you," to which Jim's face flushed scarlet red. Carter continued, "Should be back in a couple of hours. Love you."

Looking in the rearview mirror at Jim, Carter said, "When we get home, we'll let the dogs decide whether or not you have honest bones."

This time blood left Jim's face at the mention of dogs assessing his guilt or innocence. Ken piled on. "Come on, Carter, nobody we ever caught has passed the test." Seeing the fear in Jim's eyes, Ken decided to back off, lest the dogs mistake the scent of abject terror for the scent of guilt. "Just kidding," he added.

The vehicles came to an impasse near the base of the mountains with the roadway split so widely that no vehicle could pass. "We'll have to step over it and walk from here," Jim announced.

"Are we going to need light?" Ken asked.

"Depends on how far you want to go back. It can get pitch black," Jim responded.

"I'll grab a lantern," Ken said.

Behind them, black smoke from the restaurant fire had gained momentum and was already consuming the attached office and threatened to engulf the two separate buildings comprising 77 rooms beyond the pool.

Fifteen minutes later, the group reached the large cave mouth. Jim led them inside the area once occupied by dozens of men for decades. Trash of all conceived manner littered the floor and a large fire pit stood farther in.

"I'll bet you never got any smoke from your fires," Wei said.

"Uh, actually, no. We got lots of heat, though," he replied.

To no one in particular, Wei said, "If you want to build a hot, smokeless fire outside, you pull out dirt to make a fist-size hole maybe eight inches. You start another hole maybe a foot away and do the same thing, then connect the two underneath. You stack your twigs and sticks onto one of the holes and light the fire. Because smoke is created by incomplete combustion, you will get no smoke because the fire is fed by oxygen from two sides, hence complete combustion. It's the same thing here, except this is a horizontal hole and not a vertical hole."

Jim stared at the woman. "Does she always talk like this?"

The other four men said almost in unison, "Pretty much."

Jim pointed down the hill to the west toward the watercourse and said, "The river comes close enough for us to get water and a cold bath."

Carter and Ken were familiar with the meandering river as it zig-zagged throughout the valley, frequently hundreds of yards across in places, originating from numerous springs. The river once served to treat visitors to rafting and other water sports activities.

The cave mouth presented a dark opening that

widened the deeper one entered. A relatively steep incline required careful negotiation by the climbers to avoid backsliding. Once inside the cave mouth, to the entourage, Jim said, "Kody used to stay by himself a lot, back in the curve of the cave where he slept. You never knew when he would come out and check on us."

"Why don't you show us," Ken requested and followed with the light as the group migrated back in the cavern to where it narrowed and began to curve to the left. Ken held the light up high and only saw a level area on the ground and a jumble of rocks of varying sizes to one side with footprints leading to the rocks. He set down the lantern while the others watched to see what he had in mind. Rolling large and small rocks away, he reached down and pulled up a large, hefty leather bag with a draw string. Holding it up, he asked, "Any guesses?"

"Cocaine," offered Gregor, as though it were his word of the day.

"He didn't do drugs," Jim said. "He didn't drink much either. He might have thought somebody would jump him if he let down his guard, which would happen. He did take off a lot, though, to go scavenging or safe cracking, I guess."

Ken said, "Let's go back outside into the sunlight. We can open it there."

Ken set the bag on the flat granite surface that defined the entrance. He opened it and spilled out the contents to display hundreds of gems, most of which were in settings. Diamonds, rubies, emeralds and sapphires lay before them, inlaid into gold pendants, along with broaches, rings, and tennis bracelets; a ring with a central diamond surrounded by rubies, another with central sapphires surrounded by diamonds; nothing too big and clunky, everything on the finer side, only a few loose gold chains interwoven among the pile like noodles in a stir fry.

"Beats the stamp collection I had when I was a kid," Jay said.

"Did you know this was here?" Gregor asked Jim.

"No, but we all suspected the guy had something going on back here. Nobody wanted to risk their life to check it out so we left it alone. After we moved to the hotel restaurant, he said he was going to some truck stop out in Flag to live for a while and coordinate with others for the attack and left us alone. He probably took the gems with him, but after we were gone, looks like he hid them here again because there was nobody to snoop anymore."

Gregor said, "To me, the main point is: Why steal them from him? What do you do with the things? The answer is, nothing you can do. Kody might have been crazy, but he wasn't stupid. He knew they had no value, but sometimes a person steals because it's in their blood as much as is collecting the gems in the first place. And he housed a den of thieves."

Carter thought of Kody having a gemstone fetish, like somebody hooked on chocolate, cheese, or cocaine—his version of a hoarder.

Wei said, "Here's a fun idea. How about we get a

couple hundred mailing envelopes and put, say, one-to-three of these trinkets in each, seal the envelopes, put them all on a table and at breakfast, let everybody pick an envelope at random. We'll make up a few extra just in case or maybe a special one for a grand prize drawing. They can do what they want with their loot. They can trade or wear them, put 'em into artwork, whatever."

"I can see a cottage industry starting up in jewelry repair," Jay said.

"You were going to say something, Jim?" Carter asked.

The captured man replied, looking up goggle-eyed from the glittering mass, "I think I've been hanging around with the wrong crowd."

Looking at the display reminded Carter of a small box of mixed gems he had presented to Jess early in their relationship. She still wore one of the rings as a pendant around her neck. In one sense, those were one-time treasures without value, similar to the stacks of money she and Jay had discovered in the shipping trunks.

With ample help, Ken gathered and replaced the gems back in the bag, drew the opening tight and handed it to Wei.

"Make it happen," he grinned.

16

Upon receiving the call from Carter, Jess rang the large bell in the code denoting emergency meeting.

Twenty minutes later, citizens returned to their duties. A full dozen of them, men and women who belonged to the gun club, returned to their duties bearing weapons, either with holstered handguns or a rifle slung over one shoulder.

In addition, eight dogs, one of Carter's secret weapons, received instructions to patrol the forests day and night to look for strangers. Stingers constituted the other secret weapon. Any intruders would not know about the terrible insects and would not have protection against them, unlike the citizens of Sekah City who layered their skin with the oil each morning as a ritual. Many chose to wash it off by soaking in the hot springs only to reapply it in the morning.

If an attack were to occur, it would most likely be at dawn and would occur simultaneously from several directions. Heavy weapons were not expected because the enemy wanted the compound intact. In order to prevent a surprise massacre, armed guards would be posted around the meeting hall during meal time when the largest concentration of citizens was in one place. Based on the map found on the wall in the underground shooting range, new sources of entry into their compound had been defined, which were now covered.

Upon their return, Ken locked their prisoner in a room in the residence hall until a decision could be made regarding his disposition. Ken asked Jim to remove his shoes and hand them over. "It's an insurance policy," he explained. He also explained that if Jim behaved himself, there might be a positive disposition to his case.

Jim's attendants received instructions to release him every eight hours for no more than 20 minutes after providing food and water. At dawn, Jim had decided to go his own way. Ramming his shoulder against the door several times, he broke the latch and escaped running barefoot.

Hearing the noise, other residents saw him run from the building in the direction of the road leading toward Sedona. Apparently, he had no inclination to brave the dark forest barefoot. One of the residents hurried to the home that housed Jess and family to inform them of Jim's escape. Still in possession of Jim's shoes at home, Ken gave them to Carla and Riki to smell, whereupon Jay and Jess instructed their dogs to hunt for the man. Jay led them to the path Jim had reportedly taken and the two hunters were sent after him to cash in on the insurance policy.

Twenty minutes later the dogs scratched at the door wanting to get let back in. Already dressed, Jess and Jay washed the blood from the dogs' snouts. Thus far, no alarm had been given by either human or animal sentry during the night who were posted at specific locations.

In the early evening hours of the following day, the dogs heard the sound of a high-flying drone that escaped the ears of humans. None could fathom the reason for the disturbance. At that time, Wei was working at the turkey farm collecting and cleaning eggs accompanied by Riki. The dog's incessant barking drew her attention. Letting her pet outside, she followed its gaze upward. It took her several moments to find the drone, a black speck set against white clouds, struggling for stability in the gusting wind at perhaps 200-300 feet altitude. Apparently, the object, while trying to fly in a circular pattern, had great difficulty in maintaining any semblance of a true course, rocking like a spinning top ready to fall. In another instant, the speck disappeared off to the west.

They're coming, a final check. We'll be sure to thank them for giving us warning, Wei thought, doubting whether the camera on the drone had captured anything other than sky and forest for all its efforts.

Like the gang that couldn't shoot straight, the first

the attack came the next morning. It began when a running man carrying a rifle came out of the forest near the residence hall with a dog bearing down on him and her mistress close behind. The man turned to fire at the large dog who was already airborne and hit him full in the chest knocking him to the ground. The rifle went flying and the dog's mistress quickly finished the job, putting half the rounds from her magazine into the man's body even as her pet ravaged its foe.

More distant screams could be heard with single gun and rifle shots accompanied by semi-automatic rifle fire and occasional yells.

Annie's dog had treed a man who sat on a limb 10 feet above the ground. Annie was about to call her dog back to prevent her from getting shot when the man suddenly screamed in pain, slapping at his neck where a stinger had just buried its eggs beneath his skin. At the same moment, the dog made the single leap and clamped her teeth onto the man's foot so hard the man might have thought he had stepped into a bear trap. The weight of the 80 pound dog pulled the hapless victim to the ground and before Annie could get there, her pet began to tear at the screaming man's face. Tempted to let her protector finish the job, she did so instead by putting a number of rounds into the attacker. No need to clean up afterward, the forest creatures would have the corpse stripped to the bone by morning.

Four men came in from the south side where Carter and Jay had stationed themselves laying in the forest debris completely unseen. Seen from a distance, their moves appeared to be professional. They spread out, exhibiting a wariness at each step, weapons raised ready to fire, looking for trip wires at the same time. Aside from distant shouts and gunfire, the night remained silent.

Lying next to Jay, Riki's ears perked and he growled. Jay stayed him and instructed his dog to circle around and chase the men toward them. If they fired and missed, the men would disappear from view. Riki's move would keep them off balance so they wouldn't pay attention to what lay ahead, only express concern about the hound coming in from behind.

Skilled and trained in the art of avoidance, the dog circled as instructed, found the men and barked. Dodging and bounding from side-to-side, the animal avoided shots fired at him, always driving the men forward and together like a cattle dog driving a herd into a pen.

After a single minute of this, one of the men yelled for them to split up. Riki and Jay went after two that went to the left. Carter was about to go after the others when Carla appeared at his side, followed by Jess who slid on her belly next to him followed by a second dog, one of Carla's more aggressive fully-grown offspring. Both dogs had blood on their snouts.

"Ken said to tell you they have an armed troop carrier coming in from the east," Jess whispered. "They're coming in from all sides, but so far we have no losses."

Carter explained their situation and said, "You and the dogs go after the two on this side. I'll help Jay. We'll get back to Ken as soon as we can."

"Bad men over there. Go kill them," Jess commanded, immediately following the dogs who sprinted off to where she pointed with one hand, weapon in the other. All the animals had been smeared with bug oil to keep the stingers away. Not so the enemy who found themselves trying to swat the buzzing insects, which, in turn, had already found their flesh in which to lay their eggs, causing screams of pain. Normally rare to find, the stingers had found fresh prey with all the unprotected men at their behest. A green had dropped from a disturbed tree to fall onto the neck of one assailant, immediately burrowing beneath the skin, releasing tissue-dissolving acid as it did so.

Only seconds behind the dogs, Jess found the assailants on the ground with two frenzied dogs snapping at them finding purchase each time they caught flesh, shaking their heads as they did no. Jess calmly watched for a several seconds, then walked forward and put several rounds into each of the fallen men. She inserted a fresh magazine into her weapon and thought to find Carter, deciding instead to return back to base where Ken might need some assistance.

Reaching the southern greenhouse, Jess heard her name called and turned to find Carter and Jay some distance behind her. Riki had preceded them to lick Jess's hand and nuzzle the two other dogs. All three animals paced and circled anxiously, awaiting further commands.

Carter approached and said, "We need to send the dogs out again on their own" at which time he did just that.

The trio found Ken waiting for them, near the easternmost portion of boulders ringing the compound. He explained that an armored vehicle got stuck in the ditch trap his team had dug across the road some 200 yards away. Covered with sheets of drywall and dirt, the invisible trap would defeat all but the most versatile vehicle once it nose-dived into it. "Gregor already took out the guy in the back manning the 50 cal machine gun and I put enough rounds into the windshield to fracture it. Nobody can see out from the front. They're not going anywhere." Ken pointed to Gregor who lay atop the largest boulder behind a sniper's rifle and scope.

"How many do you think are in there?" Carter asked, chancing a look through the boulders.

"Maybe between six and ten. I say let them rot. If they show, we shoot."

"If anybody holds up a white flag, shoot the hand holding the flag," Jess said. "Jim already taught us that rehabilitation is not an option."

Carter looked at this cold, hard woman and wondered whether he had trained her to be this way or whether her own perspective on life had brought her to conclusions she hadn't discussed with him. She was right, of course. You either cut out every cell of the cancer, or it will show up later to kill you. Who was he to argue with the re-appointed mayor?

When darkness fell, members of the gun club lay in the vegetation of either side of the roadway, each wearing night vision goggles supplied by the weapons cache at the Flagstaff warehouse. Two hours after nightfall, a vehicle door on the north side of the carrier slowly opened and two armed men slowly and cautiously stepped out, closing the door behind them.

A fusillade of gunfire erupted to cut down the men before they could take two steps followed by rounds sent through the bullet-proof windows, all of which became fractured. Two hours later, a door on the north side of the carrier opened with similar results. The position of the vehicle guaranteed that all the occupants would be crammed in the back, down low, sliding toward the front with nobody in the driver's compartment.

At dawn, a hand waving a white flag appeared out one of the shattered windows. Carter took his shot. The flag dropped to the ground and the hand was retracted minus several fingers.

"I say they throw out their weapons next," Ken conjectured, lying next to Carter.

An hour later numerous rifles, handguns, and knives followed Ken's prediction as two doors opened slightly and the weapons got tossed. "I say one of them is keeping a handgun for emergencies," Carter offered.

"Yep, there's always one, isn't there?"

"Won't do them any good. Nobody's going near

them."

"Nope."

Another white flag got waved and another man lost a hand.

When a dog and its master would return to camp, Jess would send out the dog again until all eight worked as a team, weaving, circling, smelling, looking for a bad man. When one was found by a single hunter, he was attacked from the side or the rear, as a dog would freeze upon seeing its prey, slowly, step-by-step move in closer, until the attack. The sound would be picked up by the others and those nearby came in to ensure the man posed no further threat. The pack continued its search through hundreds of acres, occasionally finding a man running away, catching him, searching again.

After two more hours the eight warriors returned to the compound to find their masters either in the meeting hall eating, or outside the compound watching a formerly armed vehicle rot of its own accord.

Ken offered, "Our volunteers will be happy to watch the truck that went nowhere. Hey, maybe we can get Gregor to write a song about it. We'll keep an eye on it till tomorrow, then I'll toss a tear gas canister inside and see what happens."

"I'm getting hungry," Carter said, and began walking toward the meeting hall when a shot rang out. He looked up to see Gregor load another round into the rifle.

"What's he doing?" Carter asked.

"Practicing," Ken answered.

"Tell him not to shoot the tires, we're going to need to haul that thing away in a couple of days."

Ken pulled out his radio and passed on the message to the sharpshooter who kept his eye on the target while giving a thumbs up sign.

17

Several days later, Gregor and Ken towed the troop carried and its cargo to some undesignated location and then volunteers repaired the road. In a great show of appreciation for the community effort, Wei told of the great find of gems and the upcoming drawing to be held one week hence. It would take time to make a store run for the envelopes of varying sizes and to insert gems and trinkets in each. This created an air of expectation and positive excitement, a great counterbalance to the trauma of warfare. Not a single person on their side lost their life, although Annie complained that her trigger finger was sprained from overuse.

Dogs were permitted to run freely in search of bad men as a preventive measure during this time until Carter gathered his team of Jay and Wei, Jess, and Gregor. He said, "Now that the dust is settled, I want us to go down to Cottonwood. I want to look at one more thing we didn't have time for last time we were there."

On the drive, he began to ponder. There had been too much darkness and negativity befall them lately. If he had his druthers, he'd rather have none of it instead of having to fight fire with a bigger fire.

True to form, when he looked at it a different way, he saw a pendulum swinging two ways by presenting good fortune. The accidental finding of the cook stove in the loft led to the discovery of an evil person in their midst and an explanation for the illness many had suffered. The down side was the finding of the cocaine which led to the temporary addiction an entire city and the death of their doctor, yet might still be used in a constructive manner.

In addition, the poisonings brought about by Brenda's actions gave them a means to dispose of their many enemies without a shootout that would have been fatal to the community and doubtless, would have led to his own death. It also punctuated their need to build a safer city, which is currently driving him to collect the rest of the panels, a possession with no comparison in the history of the world.

The accidental discovery of Kody Davis and his crew in the restaurant alerted them to an impending attack and eventually saved them all. It also led to the finding of keys that unlocked the vast warehouse which would, forevermore, supply the community with food, clothing, and tools—no small discovery.

The finding of Kody's bag of jewels opened the door to an exciting period of time in the community.

New plays would be spawned with gemstones as a theme.

Even the sacrifice of his Mercedes got traded for the recovery of two panels and the saving of a large portion of their fresh food supply.

Yin and Yang.

18

Carter had no intention of moving his people into Jim's old cave. He had bigger and better plans. Twenty minutes later, he forced open the door to the local Walmart store and announced, "You are looking at 40,000 square feet awaiting occupancy. The ceiling has not collapsed from snow weight. I know, go figure. There is also a small eating area where they made hamburgers and hot dogs. Indoor heat will be a major problem facing us, but not so much if we only occupy a small portion of the store."

Everyone looked in awe at the immensity of the store. It still contained everything Walmart had to offer, as far as light would permit them to see. Gregor asked, not as a challenge, but as a point of curiosity, "If you mean all of us moving in here, why are we still upgrading our city?"

Carter responded, "Call it a combination of trying to stay alive during a series of crises, and easy-fix solutions."

Changing the subject to bring an upbeat note to the conversation, he added, "Here's more good news. We're far enough away and above the Verde River that the flooding didn't affect the property. The river flows every day of the year. Bass, catfish, bluegill and trout are in abundance. There are wind turbines galore in this city, some of which are standing. They're movable and repairable. We are also close enough to construct some large water wheels to generate enough power to overcome the resistance we can expect from the length of cable necessary to reach us. There are also other intact dwellings on high ground near the river available for whatever we want to make out of them. This is my choice of city for us to move to."

"You know Jess is going to want a hospital to work in," Jay contributed.

"She may need to check into one, if those headaches of hers continue. When I left her, she had a cool compress over her eyes."

Carter went to the glove box and pulled out a map, which he spread on the ground, placing rocks on the corners to ensure the wind wouldn't blow it away.

"Look, I honestly think we can make a good try at getting the rest of those panels from UL-One. I'm talking about all of them. Not to make a bad pun, but it's called 'diamonds in your own back yard'."

"There's a phrase with a broad sweep," muttered Wei.

Pointing to the map, Carter continued, "Use of

the pass is gone forever, so I marked a different route. From Flagstaff, we take US Highway 40 west to State 93, then hook southeast to Phoenix, a total of about 280 miles. If we average 35, we can make it in eight hours. In addition to the big truck to do the heavy lifting, we'll need the van for light carries, and a SUV for running around. This is a serious major project. If the truck breaks down, it's goodbye panels for this trip. It's a crap shoot because we have no idea if any road we travel on will be passable. The only other alternative route is to travel east into New Mexico, then go south and hook around. That's a 900 mile trip, figure 25-30 hours of driving one way."

Ken rubbed his chin. "I like it. The explosives are the easy part. We can get what we want from the weapons cache at the warehouse in Flag. Once we get to Phoenix, we'll find a heavy bulldozer or two and get them running. We may need to bring a couple of heavy duty batteries with us. We'll take food and water to last a half-dozen men for at least a week. Want to go, Gregor?"

"Are you kidding? Count me in," the big man replied, enthusiastically.

Carter continued, "Jay told me the top of the city is 30 feet beneath the surface of the earth. We saw some of it last time we were down. We'll finish the job. We'll blow the whole thing. Why not? After it's leveled, a lot of what's left sticking up will be the panels. They're eight feet in height, so expect to dig in order to get them. We'd better bring drums of our own reconstituted diesel fuel along for emergencies and to replace what's in the heavy equipment tanks after we drain them."

Carter began to fold the map. "It will take us a good week or more to get organized. The dogs stay home away from the heat. We'll talk about it later."

Upon their return, Gregor immediately went to ask two brothers he had grown up with to join them to complete the small team of five, a request to which they readily acceded.

After 10 days of planning, three vehicles caravanned to the warehouse. These included Ken's SUV, the van, and the U-Haul, where the team retrieved two boxes of Semtex, similar to C-4. The yellow-red malleable plastic explosive was stored in linear half-pound tubes, 20 to the crate. Ken obtained primer and detonating cords along with booster charges. Easier to transport than other explosives, such as nitroglycerin, the advantage of Semtex was that it could be shaped and molded, before being dropped down into and beneath the rubble of the city to assist in its further collapse.

Not having seen the recent condition of the city, Ken was uncertain about the way the explosives would be used. A combination of different types would be better than having to rely on a single one. Reading the code list, he directed the team to a section designating mortars and shells. He selected an M2 mortar, collecting several cases of shells along with it. He explained to the anxious recruits, "This is a short-range weapon. It launches explosive rockets at a variable trajectory, depending on the angle you proscribe. It is set up on a baseplate with a bipod support you can move to adjust the angle of elevation. It's a simple weapon without moving parts. You drop in a shell into a tube. A pin at the bottom of the tube acts like a firing pin of a gun and strikes the shell which acts like a large bullet with an explosive component. Some mortars shoot explosive shells several kilometers away. I chose this one because of its short-range capabilities of 200 to 350 yards."

He really wanted the RPGs and their launchers. Unfortunately, the crates were three-deep beneath other crates. The rocket propelled grenades had an effective range of 500—900 yards; in their case, it would have been a simple point and shoot exercise—straight line fire of less than 200 yards compared with an arc of varying heights and distances described by a mortar round. To access the RPGs would require the use of forklifts, which would not start after all these years. Given a forklift would start, maneuvering crates around in the semi-darkness would be foolhardy.

When the caravan stopped at a rest stop half way down US 93, the heat became a heavy weight, blinding at the same time. Not yet noon, the dash temperature gauge read 105 degrees. By four-o'clock it would be over 120. The constant years-long high pressure dome engulfing the central portion of the state remained alive and well. The drive to this point had been dangerous. Open stretches of uncluttered, unmarked highway tempted one to speed, until a pothole or a split across the roadway showed up out of nowhere, large enough to destroy a vehicle and its driver.

Four hours later, the caravan arrived at Ken's house. Carter called Jess to inform them of their arrival. Over the next two hours, the crew cleaned and reorganized the lower portion of the home and two generators were unloaded from the truck and taken to the garage. Extension cords ran to the upright fans, the evaporative coolers, lamps and refrigerator. The team transferred food from a large food cooler to fill the refrigerator/freezer in the kitchen with meats, eggs, cricket powder, fruits and vegetables—supplies to last for a week, if conservation were practiced.

Work accomplished for a long day, five men sat at the kitchen table for a dinner of turkey sandwiches. Ken asked Carter, "Here's a dumb question. After all the times we came down here, why didn't we ever take this route instead of going over the nightmare pass?"

"Because we're old and set in our ways and we're not too bright," Carter replied, speaking from the heart.

In a rare moment of philosophical reflection, Ken offered, "I sure hope life is more than a collection of regrets, because that's all I have when I try to get to sleep anymore."

Carter offered, "Figure a lot of them represented choices you made with the best information you had at the time. You can't short yourself for that. My father used to tell me the grass had a way of looking greener on the other side of the fence, except, all too often, the fence was made of barbed wire you were too blinded by desire to see. When you got to the other side, you found yourself ripped to shreds wondering what the hell the fuss was all about."

In a total about face, one of the volunteers asked, nervously, "Won't the Semtex explode in the heat?"

Ken shook his head quickly at the sudden about face, as a cow's hide shuttered to chase off a fly. He answered, "No. It will be fine. It's almost identical to C-4. You can hit it with a hammer and shoot it with no problem. We call it a soft explosive."

Turning back to the issues at hand, he instructed, "Water will be our big issue. The commodes will work if you pour a bucket of water down them after use. We'll have to find a source of water tomorrow. We'll concentrate on cooling down the bottom portion of the home, sleep and eat here, and close off the rest of the house.

"And, I brought a nice big bottle of hooch, if anybody wants some," he concluded.

"That's funny, so did I," Carter said.

Not familiar with the term, the other three had quizzical looks to which Carter said, "You'll find out. Let the sun burn it off tomorrow."

"Now let's see if this works." Puzzled by Ken's statement, the four followed him out of the kitchen to hear him announce, "TV ON." The large wall TV came to life as the newcomers gasped, already awed by the size of the home and the enormity of the project.

Ken offered, "We have two features tonight. We can watch *The San Diego Zoo,* or, we can watch the end of the world, as recorded, in part, by the Wei and my dear wife, Beth."

19

Planning each move step-by-step, the first order of business dictated the job site be visited. Less than an hour later, five people stood at the edge of a hole in the ground measuring a mile in circumference and 40 feet deep where they stood. Below them lay dirt combined with concrete, rebar, and an occasional panel jutting upward. Looking across, degrees of collapse presented themselves like posturing stalagmites, with the fence encompassing three sides of the pen bent into obtuse angles, testing the steel.

Carter chanced glance at Gregor, who stood looking forlorn, with an arm around the shoulders of his friends.

After a couple of long minutes, Ken said, "Gregor, unload the van and take someone with you to find us water."

"When in doubt, go to the source. If you want water, go to the bottler," Carter had said. An earlier search of an old phone book found the proper building. Although the building's skeleton remained, the two men found numerous 5-gallon glass bottles of cooler-designated water buried beneath the rubble of a roof and loaded them into the van. Several were returned to Ken's house, the remainder taken to the worksite.

The men set up a large Triple A rated insulated camping tent for their frequent rest breaks where five of the water bottles were stored. An actual upright water dispenser had been found while searching for the bottles.

Ken and Carter walked the perimeter of old UL-One only to find that trying to use the Semtex at this stage on half the city still standing wouldn't accomplish much. The mortar would be used first. In order to access the rubble down below, a down-sloping roadway would have to be dug on more than one side with the use of heavy equipment,

"Let's call it a day, guys," Ken announced. "At sunup tomorrow we're all going practice using the big toys."

Carter saw his charges had no idea what he was talking about, but were reluctant to show their ignorance. "Ken's talking about machines that move dirt around. To get them, we'll need to take the SUV and the U-Haul for tools and fuel. On a previous visit, we saw an old abandoned worksite that has the equipment we need. We're on no schedule except to keep out of the sun as much as possible, so let's go home and watch TV."

By 10::00 a.m. the next morning, after three hours prepping two yellow steel dinosaurs, Ken fired up an earth mover and Ken started a large front-end loader, preparing to follow their three assistants 20 miles south to part out a dead city.

Carter parked to the north side and Ken to the south. Both went to work cutting, gouging, scraping and moving tons of sand and caliche clay from the desert, each with one or two partners, who practiced operating the machines.

At the end of the third morning of earth moving, two roadways led down to the pile of rubble. The following day, the machines reached the bottom and began moving and tossing the remains of the city to expose the panels. These were hand-picked and trudged through the debris to be placed on one of two piles at opposite sides of the hole at the base of each new ramp.

By the end of the fifth day, over 30 panels lay stacked in each pile. It became a simple matter of tying them off, leaving a good length of nylon cord that could be used to tow the feather-weight collection up the hill to be placed in the rear of the truck.

The hot work had been grizzly due to the discovery of clothing and bones, and the level of dust generated necessitated the wearing of a mask. Damp bandanas and hats assisted in the cooling process with frequent breaks mandatory.

Before setting up the mortar on its base and bipods some 250 yards to the west of the dead city, all the vehicles were moved out of the line of fire. Only the tent remained. Carter explained, "Generally, you want to set the angle between 45 and 80 degrees, depending on how far you want to shoot. I would recommend against shooting straight up."

Ignoring the chuckles, Carter announced, checking the elevation of the weapon, "I got dibs on the first shot. Gregor, drop in the first shell and stand back."

He did as requested, waiting for the master to show his stuff. One second later, the tent exploded. Everyone broke out into laughter, thinking it hilarious, except for Carter, until everyone fell silent. Trillions of particles from disintegrated 5-gallon water bottles reflected and refracted the sun's rays, offering melding and free-flowing rainbows, a cloud of color upon shifting kaleidoscopic fluxes of rainbows high in the air. The huge mass hung suspended for long seconds before a slight breeze caught it, pushing it to one side, a living, breathing entity brought out of retirement to express itself, showing off, before disappearing forever.

Exhaling, Ken said flatly, "I thought we had too much water."

One of the volunteers offered, "Not to worry. We kept a spare bottle in the van for emergencies. That'll cover us till we reload at home."

"Party's over. Let's raise her up another five degrees to get some distance," Ken said, making the necessary adjustments on the two support legs.

After five rounds, the group walked over to inspect their work. Several of the missiles hit in the already collapsed portion of the city. The angle would have to be raised yet again.

After another five rounds, the remaining portion of the city had been hit and more panels lay exposed, waiting for pickup. The Pen, however, refused to collapse, and appeared to be reinforced, somehow.

"We don't need anything coming down on us while we're working, so we'll use the Semtex tomorrow to finish off the work and go home. I'm missing mama's home cooking."

At sunup, Ken and Carter shaped a half dozen Semtex explosive units and placed them at the edges of the Pen where the structure showed separation from the earth, but refused to fall, despite being hit by mortar fire. He inserted the detonators and wired each to a control box. The group moved back up the mountainside, protector by boulders, while Ken flipped six switches a half-second apart. Each explosive unit expanded to thousands of times its size and brought down the flooring, roof, and fence surrounding the Pen.

When the dust settled and the group walked to the edge of the crater, it became clear why the Pen resisted falling. Gottlieb had added more panels, both vertically and horizontally beneath it to ensure stability. Over and above what panels already loaded and expected to obtain, another group of six could be added to the bounty.

Within hours, the refugees from a dead city would soon have enough panels to construct an outdoor building. Once constructed, it would be safe from the elements and large enough to house their entire population with room to spare, using the barest amount of energy necessary for heating.

Carter's gut, his experience and innate sense of awareness, caused him to be suspect of the recent warming trend. If his feeling were to come true, it might possibly be the last building standing on the planet.

Better make hay before the sun stops shining, he thought, not for the first time.

PART THREE

1

The crickets continued to chirp with the wrong tempo and the dogs remained skittish even when the aftershocks had abated. These events occurred because the unusually warm weather caused the water in the Pacific to evaporate faster. As the warm, moist air rose, other air rapidly swirled in to replace it and the Coriolis effect from the rotation of the earth resulted in the counterclockwise swirl typically found in the northern hemisphere. A hurricane developed and slowly built energy to a Category 5 as it moved in to the west coast of the North American Continent. Rain clouds formed and the 15 mile per hour wind pushed them ahead of the main storm body. The friction of the rapidly rotating air mass on the water caused the formation of positive ions which were detected by creatures more sensitive to them than man.

During her morning inspection of the sky, Jess noticed a number of troubling signs: clouds were moving in from the west, their density increased along with wind velocity, the clouds appeared to be in bands as the mass pushed eastward, and the pattern appeared to rotate counterclockwise from south to north. At breakfast, she announced another emergency storm warning: a hurricane would soon be upon them. The fact that their community lay hundreds of miles from the coast had little bearing on the reality of the situation, because many inches of ocean water could be expected to dump onto the earth even hundreds of miles beyond them. Carter dispatched crews to lock the water wheels and wind turbines in place. A raging and overflowing river could be expected. And so could a few days of starvation.

The rain began in earnest in the middle of the third night and fell continuously for 36 hours, then settled for intermittent downpours for another two days. The waterwheel serving the Big House survived, but the storm waters tore loose one of the wheels serving Sekah City to sweep it downstream. Miraculously, both greenhouses survived the onslaught thanks to the windbreaks established through Carter's efforts.

Once the storm has passed, Carter and Ken walked down to the riverbank to help Jay and Wei with the fish screens. It had been Jay's idea to leave an opening at the side of the fish screen where it abutted the wall of river at the home base in order to enable some of the fish to escape, only to be trapped at the downstream site. This provided for two catch sites in case one of them gave way, a likely possibility once the fish stacked up and the added water pressure caused the supports to break lose.

Jay saw the airplane first come in from the west while looking off to the white mammatus clouds, countless swollen bellies like cows' udders beneath the cumulonimbus, indicating a strong storm might be approaching. From beneath them, a black spot moved with the pink underbellies of the clouds serving as a backdrop. He pointed. "Somebody tell me I'm not looking at a plane."

Ken took one look and ran to the truck, returning a moment later with the binoculars Carter kept in the glove box. He took a moment to find the plane, spent another several seconds adjusting the focus, then passed them to Carter, who ensured Jay and Wei both had a chance to get a closer look. Wei passed them back to Ken.

Following the plane's progress, Ken said, "It's definitely coming from west traveling a little southwest. It's not the same one we saw last year, and it's flying supersonic. What do think?"

Carter reported, "Whoever it is has to be brave. That cloud formation looks nasty. I'd put the altitude at maybe 30,000 feet. Wait a second, it's a prop jet. How can a prop jet fly supersonic? Oh shit," he exclaimed. Without explanation, he passed the binoculars back to Ken, while Jay and Wei watched the plane while paying rapt attention to the commentary.

The plane came more directly toward them. Ken zoomed in as close as he could without losing the object. Any sudden movement would be magnified in terms of distance lost from the target. Watching him, the others froze in place, said nothing while Ken breathed shallowly, speechless, totally focused on the moment. At last, as the plane passed directly overhead, he handed the binoculars back to Carter, who, with an experienced hand, quickly backed off the zoom, found the plane and smoothly zoomed in again, following it completely until it disappeared beyond the horizon. "Fucking Russian plane, flying low," he announced.

"TU-95?" Carter asked Ken.

"Yep, looks like it," Ken agreed. He explained to the confused couple awaiting explanation. "The TU-95 is the renowned Russian Bear. The full name is Tupilov-95 and believe it or not, it's propeller-driven and the first of such to fly at supersonic speeds because it has jets behind it. The damn thing can carry twice the load of a B-52 and has twice the range. This is a very expensive bomber."

Carter looked at Ken, who had found himself a comfortable spot on which to recline on the gravel of the river bank, with hands held behind his head, propping it, contemplating.

Wei asked, "Okay, if it's Russian, where did it come from?"

Ken said, "Unknown. The nearest large Russian base is Vladisvostok on the east side of the continent. Don't ask what it's doing here."

Carter added, "Its range is a good 10,000 miles. Russian jets used to fly into Alaskan airspace all the time, maybe 3000 miles each way from their big base in Vladivostok. If Vlad is the home base, the Tu-95 probably wouldn't make it home from here without refueling, considering it's still flying west, never mind it passing through any air defenses we have left and never mind what it's doing this far south."

Carter asked, "So, where is it going? How much life is present where it came from? Is this an invasion? Why invade anything anymore? Why isn't anybody chasing it?"

Wei said, "I don't get any of it."

Carter pretended to pull a pencil from his pocket, and replied, glibly, "Really. Let me write that down." Then he added, "Tell you what, though, let's check with Beth to see if she can find anything. This is too important." At that, the quartet hurried to the meeting hall to find both Beth and Jess, and asked them to stop preparing dinner and for Beth to warm up her radio.

Moments later, she sat before the old Zenith TransOceanic Radio on the counter. She eschewed the use of headphones which she normally wore to avoid bothering others in the home, which included Ken, Jay and Wei, Jess and Carter, the babies, and two dogs, while they went about their own activities. At this point in the middle of the day, little activity occupied the wavebands, most of it foreign. The poor reception might not be associated with a lack of transmission, but associated with an unstable atmosphere. Or perhaps, people were tired of trying to reach others after 20 years. At the request of

Carter, she checked the frequencies associated with transmissions from Russia. Now she was receiving a two-person conversation on a single frequency, not simply an identification, a speech, or a call for help.

"I got something," Beth announced.

Wei quickly came over and the others crowded around. "It's Russian," she reported.

"Who knows Russian?" Beth inquired. "Do you? You know a lot of languages."

Wei said, "True, but Russian isn't one of them, although I know the sound of it. Try Annie. She and Gregor were born in Kiev, Ukraine. The language is similar."

"Oh, yeah. Quick, see if you can find her before we lose this," Beth urged.

"I'll go," announced Jess, who quickly ran back to the meeting hall to separate Annie from her assistants. By the time the two women arrived, Beth had turned up the volume, playing with the squelch while Annie listened intently.

At last Annie said, "Both parties mentioned several things. . . about their last nesty running away, or something like that. . . or nesty not calling home." Annie had a complete English vocabulary, although she retained a heavy accent, pronouncing the "th" sound as "t", unable to get her mouth in the right position.

"Nesty?" Ken asked.

"It's the Russian word for bear. Nobody can find it," Annie said, puzzled.

Carter exclaimed, "Tupilov-95. The Russians

and the Americans always called it The Bear. That must be the plane we saw." He quickly explained to Annie what had occurred in the skies short minutes before.

"Maybe they lost contact with it," Wei suggested.

The signal faded. Carter suggested, "Or maybe it went rogue and didn't want to call in. That's an expensive plane to lose, especially these days. Obviously, it didn't plan to return, based on its course and its range capability. It may not have gone through Anchorage at all, but took a more southern route from Russia, then came westerly. Where it plans to land is anybody's guess. Under those circumstances the Russkies would scramble their fighters to shoot it down, if necessary."

"Maybe they don't have any fighters left to scramble?" Ken suggested.

Annie held up a hand for silence and listened, as the signal regained strength. "It's a two-way conversation with a lot of 'sirs' involved. Sergei Vasilov took the plane. One of the men talking is a colonel who is very upset. He's the one asking about the bear. He says he can't contact Vasilov or anybody else to get any information. It doesn't sound like things are going well over there."

Jess started to say something when Annie held up her hand again for silence, then she put her hand to her mouth and spun around to look at the others and said, *"Neskolko yadernoye oruzhiye.* It is carrying several nuclear bombs."

The voices got weak and faded away. Beth played

with the radio for several minutes, got other stations, but lost that one.

"Where do you think the broadcast came from?" Ken inquired, totally involved, as were the others.

"Relatively close, I should think," Beth replied. "Whenever I hear anybody say the word Moscow or the Russian equivalent, for example, the signal is very weak. Anybody that far north was facing 40 below for years, never mind wind chill, which includes most of Russian, Alaska, and northern Canada."

Carter contemplated, "Which tells us they had underground storage and survival facilities. The Israelis did, even before the Big Catastrophe, and I know damn well we had at least two, not counting a hollowed out mountain in Colorado and another in Utah. Count the Chinese in as well. Maybe the plane was initially sent out to tease our air defenses in the Bering Straits, you know, to see if we even have anything, but the crew had other ideas."

"From all indications, there's still some life out there," Jay put in, attempting to be encouraging.

"And probably not all for our betterment," Carter countered, thinking about the numerous lives they had recently taken in their own small portion of the state.

Ken asked, "Beth, can you dial in any frequencies used by pilots or air traffic controllers? West of here is Albuquerque and by this time the plane is probably in northern Texas, maybe heading toward some airfield in Dallas."

Beth checked her reference book and selected

two frequencies relatively close together. In an instant she lucked out and obtained the conversation between the pilot of the Russian plane and somebody on the ground who was at Tinker Air Force Base outside of Oklahoma City challenging the plane. "The Russian wants asylum. The man on the ground is saying they had no good runway space for such a large plane and suggests they turn south some 200 miles to Dallas. They would take their chances because no communication existed between any two airfields, as far as he knew. Nor do they have any planes to offer escort."

Suddenly, the sound of static replaced the conversation.

"EMP," Ken said.

Carter explained, "Electromotive pulse—it occurs when a nuke goes off—shuts off anything electronic. Tinker was huge. It used to have everything from B 52s, to F-16s, to nukes. And if that's what happened, I'm thinking it may have hit Alamagordo, 200 miles south of Albuquerque, before it swung north. This guy Vasilov finished off what was left after the tornadoes ravaged the base."

Ken explained, "Holloman Air Force Base is, or was, in Alamagordo. It was probably the largest military base in the United States. The base included White Sands Proving Grounds, home to experimental aircraft and an assortment of missile launches, plus top secret stuff nobody ever got to know about. The Russkie may have hit that one before it hit Tinker."

"Which way is the wind blowing," Wei asked, worried about possible fallout.

"Aside from the hot bubble over the Phoenix metro area, typically southerly, away from us in New Mexico. Can't speak for Oklahoma, though," Jess replied, as the resident meteorologist. Beth had shown her videos of nuclear explosions when she had visited their home in the old days. The memory was seared into her brain forever.

Ken surmised that the air traffic controller at Tinker existed for the benefit of small planes that were likely hangered most of the time and the controller had chanced to be on station when the call came in from the Russian plane. The plane might have been trying to reach various locales along the way, using the asylum approach as a ruse in case it was detected.

For the next two hours Beth worked the radio, trying to find follow-up radio contacts along the possible flightpath of the bomber to no avail until Carter summarized, "Vasilov'ss probably running on fumes right now. Unfortunately, it doesn't sound like there is anybody to come to our rescue. We're on our own."

Upon hearing the word 'rescued' Jay broke out in a short laugh, almost a bark, then abruptly stopped. "Sorry," he said. "I don't think I ever contemplated being rescued. I mean, and go where, to some hideout underneath a mountain? No thanks. The devil you know is better than the one you don't."

"I'm not too sure I want to be rescued. From what

I've seen, as a race, we're still trying to do ourselves in," Jess offered, feeling a sense of aloneness, the loss of a fading secret hope.

Times had changed. Wei had retrieved a crate of electronics during their early visit to the warehouse for the express purpose of rebuilding Beth's radio. She offered, sadly, "I can get you more range, but I don't think it will help except to make us feel even more alone than we are. I don't know if there is any other way to find out who's out there without exposing ourselves. I think we've gone through enough exposure to last for some time, don't you agree?"

Those listening to Wei began to somberly nod in agreement until Jay asked, "Do you think there's a possibility we got photographed from anybody overflying us?"

Seeing the puzzled look on a couple of faces, he added, "If a spy satellite at 200 miles above the Earth can read the license plate on your car, an advanced plane like that one flying at mid-altitude should be able to see a ring of red boulders near a river with an assortment of vehicles parked on one side of them. Not to mention intact structures inside and outside the ring with people and dogs walking around."

Not seeing a smile on anybody's face and uncertain of Jay possibly using a sense of humor she did not fathom, Wei asked "What would be the point, unless they wanted to take out a bunch of harmless civilians?"

Jay shrugged, without a hint of mirth, "Those are questions a sane person would ask."

2

The following year, in the new Cottonwood hospital, the resident professional microscope expert,
Doctor Jessica Galloway Lawson performed her
first operation by repairing and setting a splintered
forearm, followed by her first of many deliveries,
this one by Caesarian section. In both cases, she was
assisted by Alex and A.J. In both cases, she made
abundant use of alcohol and iodine, and proper dosage of a topical anesthetic, of which she had an endless supply.

Jess also welcomed the eyeglasses Carter had obtained for her off the rotating rack at the local drug
store, which served to end her headaches.

The Mars Virus led to the destruction of civilization on Earth and instability of the planet itself.
Yet now, with the assistance of Jay Whitmore, the
only person who remembered the very beginning,
along with his wife, Wei, who watched the very
end, the most stable structure in the history of man-

kind neared completion. A newly cordoned off 1500 square foot interior section of the Walmart store joined the new structure. The rooms of the residence hall were larger than those of old for the reason that half the population opted to remain in Sedona.

Ironically, the primary components of this structure, millions of years old, consisted of that same terrible virus that still expressed its capabilities on Planet Earth, a structure destined to last countless years more, perhaps one day to be puzzled over by visiting aliens.

As the next years were to testify, the virus had only begun its work on the human mind. People would no longer require short wave radios to determine whether other survivors existed or where they might be situated.

EPILOGUE

Some five years after completion of the residence hall/meeting room complex in Cottonwood, perhaps even before, the undefined whisperings had begun. No person escaped them. Initially, the new assault of the Mars Virus on the human mind could be ignored, as easily as one ignores flagrant thoughts or dreams that arise from nowhere. Those occurred more profoundly and rapidly with Jess, Jay, and Wei because of their sider DNA.

The whisperings became more numerous over the months until slurred words could be discerned.

Jess felt herself connected to Jay and Wei in so many ways. Driving up to Sekah City from her part-time home in Cottonwood, she visited with them at her other part-time home to discuss the matter.

Jay explained, "The human body is an instant reaction machine when adrenaline pumps in a fight or flight reaction. It is also a delayed reaction machine when hormones rage at certain age. The virus hit us hard and fast to make us smarter and faster. Then it settled in. Now, after something like 25 years, it is causing further changes. This time it appears to be in the mind only, but who is to say whether it will affect our bodies."

Wei took over, "Jess, the whisperings are real voices. The three of us are better at receiving the thoughts than are others. We are telepaths who are improving every day. Give it another few months and we'll have a game plan worked out for everyone."

Jess scratched the back of her neck, trying to wrap her head around what her friends were telling her. On the surface it made sense, especially when she considered the citizenry reported hearing voices in different languages. Several months ago, perhaps as long as a year, she began to hear a person's voice, only to find no one nearby. Most frequently it occurred at night when she enjoyed a relaxed state. Over time, others reported the same occurrences. When she first mentioned it to Carter, he laughed and said that in the old world, a single complaining office worker could get the entire department involved, until the whisperings became reality for him too.

"What do we do in the meantime?" She wanted to know.

Jay said, "Don't fight it. Open your mind and accept the intrusions. That will enable us to develop faster and be in a better position to guide others when the time comes to do so."

The time did come when Jess faced a seated audience of 75 souls with several babies in tow. Behind them stood the east wall of the reconstructed interior of the Walmart store adorned with paintings of the old underground city. To her right stood the old entrance to the store attached to new the residence hall constructed almost entirely of capsid panels. Three well-placed spotlights obtained from the grand warehouse in Flagstaff served to provide ample lighting.

She'd trained hard for the past six months and passed on her knowledge to Carter and an eager Gregor, both of whom sat in the front row. Her twins, Tracy and Vincent, nearing seven years of age, sat on either side of their father. The audience knew the subject matter. Now it would find out the game plan.

Jess began, knowing an identical meeting was being held in Sedona with the other half of the population. "We believe the Mars Virus is activating itself again to provide us all with new abilities. For the most part, we are becoming telepathic. We don't know where this will end. We do know the human mind will be open as never before. We need to be proactive, but not afraid. In doing so we will save ourselves a lot of grief.

"This course is divided into several segments we have named: Coping, Finding the Off Switch, Seek and Find, Opening the Crack, Two on One, Gang Attack, Defensive Mechanisms, General Broadcasting, Target Acquisition, Sabotage, and Playing Dead."

She went on to explain each of the skills, several of which related to direct communication with others, while several related to keeping unwanted others from reading the thoughts of the sender.

She concluded by saying, "We'll meet twice a day, an hour after breakfast and an hour before dinner. Practice what we teach. Now we'll divided into three groups for our first session which will have to do with the basics of sending and listening."

Fortunately, Jess's learning curve far exceed that of the general population because of her intense study with Jay and Wei over the past months, her sider capabilities, and her one-on-one work with Carter and, to lesser extent, with Gregor.

An hour later, she answered several questions when she received a message from Jay after everyone had left. *"How did it go?"*

She returned, *"As well as could be expected. I'm concerned about some people who may need therapy and I don't know anyone who can provide it, not for this kind of thing."*

"Jess, please target your thoughts to the recipient. Everybody in the world will know what your thoughts are if you broadcast generally, Wei teased.

The following month, she began the lecture in the following manner. "Blocking is more important than sending. As more and more people come 'on line' and all of our skills become greater, there will be more communicating, which means the number of voices in your head will increase. Understand that whatever any other telepath knows or experiences is a virtual open book. Get used to it. You now stand naked. In fact, I would rather stand naked physically, than bare my insides to prying eyes. Blocking skills prevent your mind from becoming naked. It also prevents others from getting in there to possibly do damage.

"Everybody has a garbage pile inside their head. Learn to block it off, unless you don't care. That's your choice. In fact, walling off is not that difficult. It's almost as though it is a normal human defense mechanism. The other skills are harder to develop, but can be fun. The skills include what we call the Concentrating on a Safe Place and the Image. When you feel uninvited persons trying to get into your head, and believe me you will, you focus your attention on something you either love or hate. For me, I concentrate hard on cutting open broken arms and repairing broken bones during surgery."

Here the audience laughed, a necessary break in the tension. "Or try the opposite. For example, most people don't like spiders. But if you concentrate on those, anybody trying to enter your mind will become repulsed.

"We're going to split into groups of four and five. Take turns trying to block the others. We'll go around and assist." She said this knowing Ken and Beth were assisting up north even as she spoke.

During later lessons, she heard herself say, "Picture the face of the person you are sending to, that will help." "Shut off your own thoughts and block others at the same time." "Find a crack in the other's defense." "Sift through multiple senders to select a specific one."

The one thing she did not teach, which she discovered quite by accident and which she only revealed to a select few, was how to slide through the strongest defense. Unbeknownst to her at the time, she would later find out by accident how and when to destroy a mind.

It would soon become apparent that telepathic waves could not be impeded by capsid walls, inclement weather, or the Earth itself. For those who had an ear for such things, the multilingual nature of the words received pointed to persons around the world who were "coming on line." A big question voiced at the daily meetings was: "Where will it all end?"

Jess addressed this issue by describing other types of psychic phenomena, such as precognition or seeing into the short and long term future, and clairvoyance, the ability to mentally locate a person.

What she failed to mention was that when she wanted to recall the exact circumstances surrounding a specific event at a specific time, even close to birth, she could instantly retrieve the information. Her memory was becoming absolutely indelible. Frustratingly, she had no clue what to do with the newfound ability. Nor could she yet understand how to unite the minds of those out there who needed a leader, to battle against a gathering storm of darkness, and out of those she had found, other than Jay and Wei, none were siders.

Something Wei had said gave her great cause to ponder. Wei had said that once Jess gained confidence, her mental abilities would far exceed theirs. Although this concept possessed an air of majesty, it seemed to her that the marionette humans would always serve the virus master, dancing to its string-pulls. She thought it idiosyncratic that this all-conquering virus had mutated everything it touched, including whole worlds, yet had programmed the remaining human population to take another evolutionary leap. Whether this bonded them or separated them remained to be seen. She saw it as another complication that would do nothing to change human nature.

Her two children had the vocabulary of most adults and frequently attended their mother when she performed surgeries and were self-motivated to read copiously. Their mental skills could only be described as exceptional.

The dogs were another matter altogether. Carla would come to her at a thought command, just as Jess would understand her needs to go out, hunt, eat or drink, or to be loved, not in words, of course, but with impressions.

Still struggling hard to find peace with herself, Jess walked next to the rushing river with Carla in the cold evening air; wind-blown, lost in space, a feeling to which she had become accustomed. Once a little girl growing up secure in an underground city, she found herself transplanted onto the surface, transformed into a surface creature, surviving the elements, at war with evil forces. She was not the same person at all, now in her mid-twenties. She had evolved into a mass executioner and a surgeon, telepathic no less, leading a band of lost citizens toward an unknown destiny. As Carter would say, "What a shit storm."

It promised to be a lengthy one at that. She looked forward to engaging the new challenges with great expectation, mixed with a dash of trepidation. She sent a message. *The next few years should be very interesting for us, don't you think, dear?*

Carla wagged her tail, whined, and licked the hand of her mistress.